I0698934

PUNK goes HORROR

A MIXTAPE ANTHOLOGY

DEDICATION

This one's for Joey and Joe and Mick and Jeff and Joan and Billie Joe and Sid and Iggy and Chrissie and Gerard and Siouxsie and Johnny and Glenn and Mark and Adam and Stefan and Amy and...screw it...why not... freaking POPPY and everyone else who taught us that a busted lip can be worn as a badge of honor.

CHECK OUT THE
PUNK GOES HORROR
PLAYLIST THAT INSPIRED
THIS ANTHOLOGY

Tehno

A MIXTAPE ANTHOLOGY

Edited by William Sterling

Truborn Press

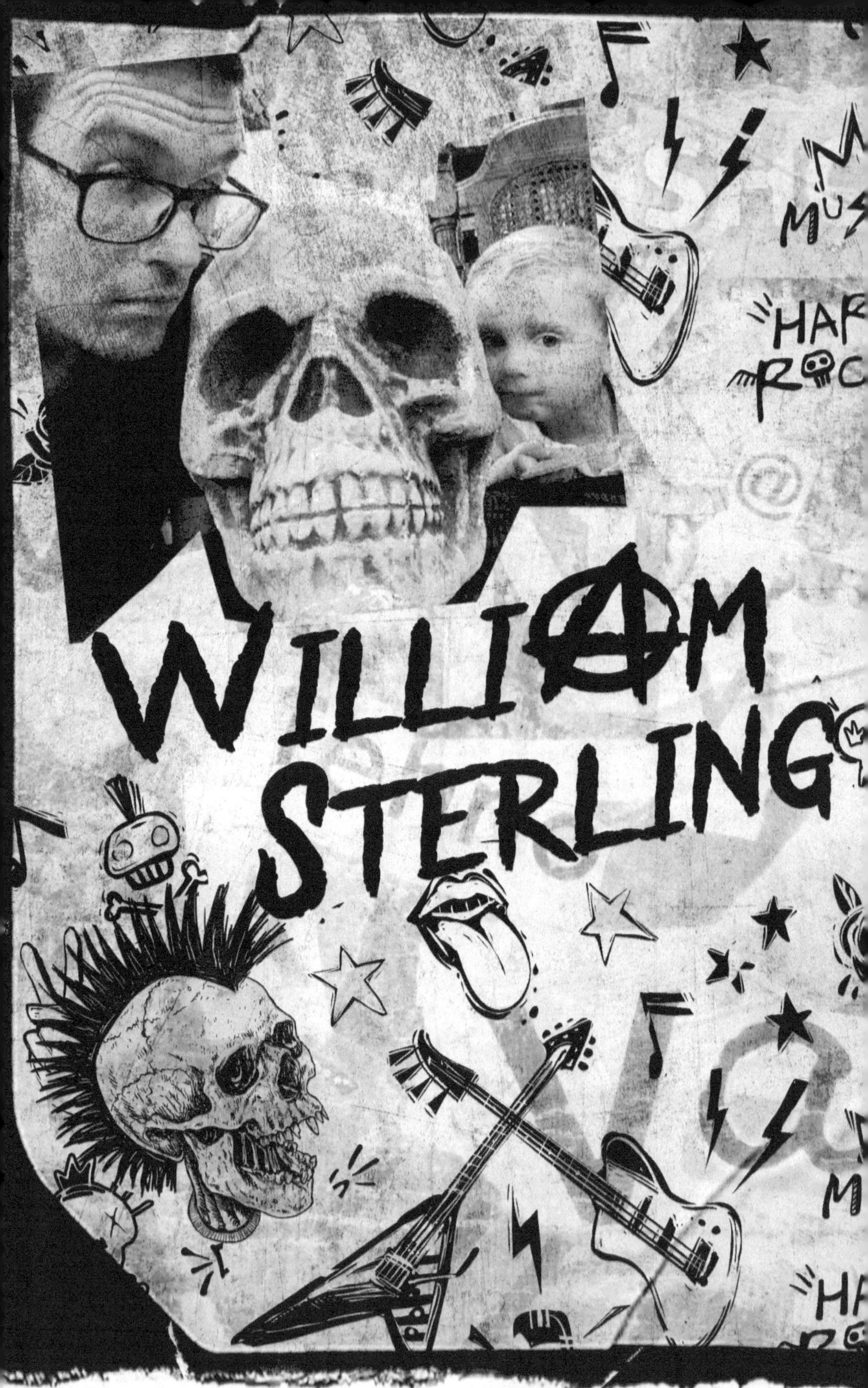

WILLIAM
STERLING

INTRODUCTION

William Sterling

There's a special kind of magic fueling cover songs, isn't there?

From the grimiest of basements to the largest of festival stages, we get to hear bands, artists, and musicians, pounding out their own interpretations of their favorite anthems from their fellow rockers. War cries of emotion, repackaged, repurposed, and kicked back at us with a whole new attitude.

And whenever it's a PUNK song in question? That attitude can come back at us in a glass bottle, a flaming shirt tail trailing behind it. A comet, streaking through the sky. A message from the working class, heaved directly into crowds of pulsing, godless anarchy.

It's hearing that BLUR snubbed your local music festival, then hearing band after band after band playing SONG 2 as a middle finger to everyone who thinks they're better than them.

It's hearing Denzel Curry covering Bulls on Parade with so much passion that even the supporting band looks a little scared.

It's knowing that the emotion behind these songs can be more important than getting every note right. More important than being "technically" correct, just so long as we get our excuse to feel something, damnit.

PUNK is a message.

Screw your standard song structures.

To hell with your thousand dollar instruments.

We've got four strings left on this six string and we're gonna make each one of them scream.

Kick a combat boot through your fancy sound systems. We've got one busted subwoofer and half a tweeter left, but they're still enough.

It is in this spirit, with our instruments tuned to the key of horror, with semicolons, periods, and punctuation marks pounded out like percussion, that the authors in this anthology have laid their own sacrifices bare atop the altar of punk rock.

There's a cadence here. A rhythm that functions as an almighty through line, connecting body horror to bass drums; rhythm guitars to psychological terrors; microphones to human monsters.

Like so many other artists, our authors have drawn inspiration from some of their favorite songs whose words, melodies, or in some cases just general vibes, struck one of those proverbial chords deep within them.

Some of our authors used this anthology as an opportunity to transport us back to their youths, recalling mixtapes, trashed car speakers, iPods, or whatever other means of musical mayhem they leaned into when they were vulnerable, or angry, or thrilled, or joyous.

Others played in the present, wielding new age bangers like sacks of bricks as they demanded that we open up the pit. Wider. Wider. All the way fucking open. And then they left us all holding our breaths in anticipation for the breakdown.

Still others just had some fun with things. Got punk rock as hell and laid it all out there.

But regardless of their wells of inspiration, in every single case, I think these covers cocked their fists back, aimed for the gut, and then swung for the fences. They laughed in the face of authority, of status quos, of the way things are "supposed to be." They pushed their mohawks up in spikes and they made some goddamn statements. I'm so proud of the collection that's come together, and I'm thrilled to share the stories that these artists have played for us.

At times it's beautiful.

At times it's messy.

And I feel like that's half the point.

So, without further ado, I'd like to invite you into our beautiful chaos.

All together, let's raise our lighters in the air. Let's throw up our rock fists if you're feeling it when we drop this. Let's clap and thrash and sing along until our lungs collapse and security drags us, still kicking and still screaming, all the way to the medical tent.

Let's burn this grungy tinder-box of a venue to the ground together.

I'm so very excited to present…

PUNK.

GOES.

HORROR.

And the lights go off.

And our first artist takes the stage.

And the screaming begins.

William Sterling
Editor of *PUNK goes HORROR*

FANTASMAGORIANA DELUXE
A Complete Edition of FANTASMAGORIANA and TALES OF THE DEAD
Eric J. Guignard

A WORLD OF HORROR

PROFESSOR CHARLATAN BARDOT'S
TRAVEL ANTHOLOGY TO THE MOST
(FICTIONAL) HAUNTED BUILDINGS
IN THE WEIRD, WILD WORLD
edited by Charlatan Bardot and Eric J. Guignard
illustrated by Steve Lines and James Gabb

Eric J. Guignard
LAST CASE AT A BAGGAGE AUCTION
with Illustrations by Steve Lines

Eric J Guignard

DARK MOON BOOKS

MORE COMING SOON!

VOLUME 4

VOLUME 6

SMELLS LIKE TEEN SPIRIT

Eric J. Guignard

It happens in low-rent apartments, motels maybe, pads where you can still pay by the hour; vestibules of solace to shoot up dreams and the sweet slide of melancholic seduction. It's raining outdoors, because it must. The sounds, a musical beat on concrete streets, on awnings, bouncing, splashing, hissing on red and violet neon lights of every dive bar and coffee shop on the strip. Those lights, even through the rain, they glow like lighthouse beacons in the gray, the fog and gloom that rolls down the street like a storm front of wraiths.

This is the hour, not at midnight, but at whatever time you're most rejected, most loathed and glum. When the world says you don't fit in, you don't conform to the square-pegged roles of social know-how. You go into that flat-tiled bathroom with its sink that drips without end, with its toilet streaked by rust and excrement, with its too-small drain corroded by grime and roach repellent. In here, a row of flickering incandescent light bulbs gives shadowbox-flashes of cobwebs and dead filaments. Dark, light, dark, light.

So you go into this bathroom and stare at yourself, at the face that once cheered, the face that once glowed bright with childlike innervation but now hangs lined and used and listless. You look three times into the mirror, and you say:

"*Teen Spirit.*

"*Teen Spirit.*

"*Teen Spirit.*"

And no claw-handed madman appears.

No vengeful demon set to slay.

That's all mainstream media bullshit.

But what *does* come is recognition that someone's smoking weed, and it's not far away. It's an aroma that's been in this room and you didn't catch its drift until now, until saying those words. There's a smell of hormonal sweat too, something that only comes from a drinking jag with friends after a late night show, and suddenly it's 4:00 in the morning, and Rainier Beer is secreting from your pores. Maybe it's the crinkled fast-food wrappers soaked in grease, maybe it's the leather of new Doc Martens or the sharp spice of fifteen types of incense oils smoldering and stinking at their bases. Maybe it's something else, something instinctual and primal that fires up the nerves, that stimulates the reactions that the mind-quacks call "Fight or Flight," and you realize the time for flight is done.

You look down then, and you've got your flannels on, and you wake up, and it's time to fucking roar.

* * *

Remember those old crooners, the black-bowtie affairs that tickled the ivories so gently it was like a siren's call, drawing nostalgic tears to cascade down every soft cheek in range? Their voices so easy and melodic, their unworried mouths forming perfect O's, while someone in attendance fingered a drained highball, and a barkeep filled it with a double Gin Rickey or maybe a French 75 for some flair. Time went by slow there, regulated by a maudlin tempo as precise as any gentleman's half-wound timepiece. Then Werner or Rosalyn might have rose and joined in for a duet, or—hold onto to the clasp of your waistcoat—little Franklin P. Jehovah be ushered in to give rendition to "Great Is Thy Faithfulness." And that could go on all night, until the lady of the evening fainted onto her velvet settee from the sheer emotional exhaustion of it all.

Then one day someone finally said, "Fuck all this."

And they plugged in an electric guitar.

* * *

There's a string of incidents in this city, destruction of civic property, misappropriation of public transportation, noise pollution, obstruction in the streets, general anarchy and carousing at all hours. Some say it's a ghost, a phantom right here in Modern Metropolis wailing the voice of the distressed.

But the police dissent.

They come. They bust heads. They make arrests. They file reports, take witness statements.

A young sergeant is called forth, John Sigford. He's asked to make a police sketch from witness testimony; he interviews them, takes a composite from credible descriptions.

"Tell me what you saw," he says to an elderly woman while readying his artist's 2B graphite pencil over a pad of paper.

The witness is wearing a blue pantsuit, and she's attractive in such toned way that comes from years of doing yoga twice a week, from eating Greek yogurt and cottage cheese for breakfast. Her short, pale hair is no-nonsense, her tight lips more so. She replies, "What I saw was dirty and unloved. You can tell, tell so much. A bad upbringing, poor choices, no moral compass. It's the delinquent ne'er-do-wells spitting on what we've built."

Sergeant John nods encouragingly. His pencil makes sharp whisking sounds as it works.

"Could you define the suspect as a familiar scene?" he asks. "A recognizable space? Was there insurrection in the heavy-lidded eyes?"

"What I saw was crude and unwholesome. Corruptible, I'd say. A bad influence on our youth, a gateway to depravity. Shaggy hair and baggy pants, cigarettes and circus hats. And this *s*for undefined change. It just doesn't make sense, I tell you!"

Sergeant John nods again, and he shows the woman what he's drawn.

It's abstract, raw and jagged, lines like screams, like Southern Blues set to the electric chair. There's a mash of bold hatches, a linear perspective that's insensible; the paper's torn through in some places, scribbled over and over itself in others. A hundred penciled Rorschach shapes are found within, and they could be horny rats or Camel Lights, or hearts shattered into a billion twinkling shards; it's just a matter of how you look at it.

"Is this it?" he asks.

"Oh yes," the woman says, rising and pointing and exclaiming. "That's it exactly, that's the culprit!"

* * *

A four-power-chord riff settles over the city, haunting the wind. Eager and hungry and adored. Residents can hear it, can feel it. Most are uneasy.

Lightning cracks.

Grocers slur lyrics in their sleep. Postmen mumble jaded poetry. Pipe fitters and dock workers find themselves introspective at union halls, searching for existential authenticity. And no one knows why, except that maybe people are pissed at the Reagan years, of the worsening income inequality, sick of the healthcare failure, sick of the education system that's broken and catering only to the privileged few who don't give two shits about it in the first place.

A bottle smashes over a bus stop bench. An amp distortion howls its baying feedback. The disaffected gather to the riff's call, finding each other, finding they're not alone. They gather and they grow.

And the voices murmur "Teen Spirit."

And the voices cry "Teen Spirit."

And the voices demand "Teen Spirit."

And the city cracks.

* * *

There's a young woman named Tawny LaMere who works at 24/7 Mart, and she hates herself for what she's lost, and she can't figure out why her high school youth and hope don't fit this twenty-four-year-old's life anymore. She feels the change, feels the rage, and looks at herself in the mirror, and she says "Teen Spirit" three times, and after that she's never seen again… Not in the way she was anyway. But she's still there, still around, this *reborn* Tawny LaMere, the one that doesn't work at 24/7 Mart anymore. The one who never did.

The one who took a different life path.

And over there's a guy named Nathan Pike, and he lost his lease, and he's crashing on a cousin's couch, until he can land a temp job in a seafood plant; he always thought he'd be a reformist fashion designer. He's alienated, isolated, trashed. He looks at himself in the mirror and he says those words, and he's given a new lot. Whatever he does, whatever he becomes, it won't involve canning air-dried sardines.

And meanwhile in the moonlit abandoned wards, heartsick mourners and daredevils of the arcane slide planchets over those telling letters of the Ouija board, and what comes back every… single… time… is *Teen Spirit.*

* * *

And Sergeant John Sigford is still doing his investigative work, trying to uncover the truth, the motive, the aggravating circumstances. But it's frustrating. This culprit, it's insidious, it's everywhere. There're a thousand leads, but none of them point to any one source. Someone, something, somehow, has upset the balance, and people are changing, the constructs of society changing, a call declared in A-Major for hippy-punk rock arms to tear down the infrastructure of apathetic suburbia.

But Sergeant John catches a clue, a fragment of verse, and the forensics lab transcribes it. Analysts puzzle at it, they run it through cross-agency data bases. They extrapolate patterns, historic precedents.

It's close, so damn close…

Then a nosey journalist comes along, catches wind of the whole thing, exposes the case. The column in *The City Times* goes to publication, and maybe it's preachy, and maybe it's trite, but it charges people, man, and it goes something like this:

> *What class of man is left outdoors in the rain, on society's back stoop like a sad, bedraggled dog? What generation of youth survives the cruel labyrinthian torments of adolescence only to find their singular exit to be blocked by an impenetrable boulder, carved by gatekeepers that decide who may be allowed to pass? So whether it's 1990 or 3052, there will always be someone oppressed, someone trampled and hurt, misunderstood, jeered and leered,*

> *trashed and clinging to the fringes of their apothecarial dream, staring at themselves in the mirror, whispering, whispering, and maybe now those voices are louder than ever who recite: "Teen Spirit."*

And so it is with Sergeant John Sigford too, when he wakes from unsettling dreams and cold sweats in the middle of the night.

He realizes he doesn't want to do it anymore.

That he's never wanted to do it.

When he was in high school, he'd wanted to be a wedding planner in Australia, and his parents had laughed, and his father socked him in the back of the head, said to "wise up and get a real job, be a man the family could be proud of."

Sergeant John feels the anger, the rebellion, and—what he finds too—is that it's a relief. It doesn't have to fester inside, eating away like the cancer that rotted his own abusive father's guts. He doesn't have to be alone and living someone else's constructs, trapped in a conformist authority of his own sufferance. He can be anyone he wants.

So he makes his way into the bathroom, and he looks at the mirror to see what he's become, and he balls his hand into a hard-knuckled fist and shatters the glass, and he falls through to the other side, and he finds himself.

And that chanting, beautiful, timeless chorus grows louder by one.

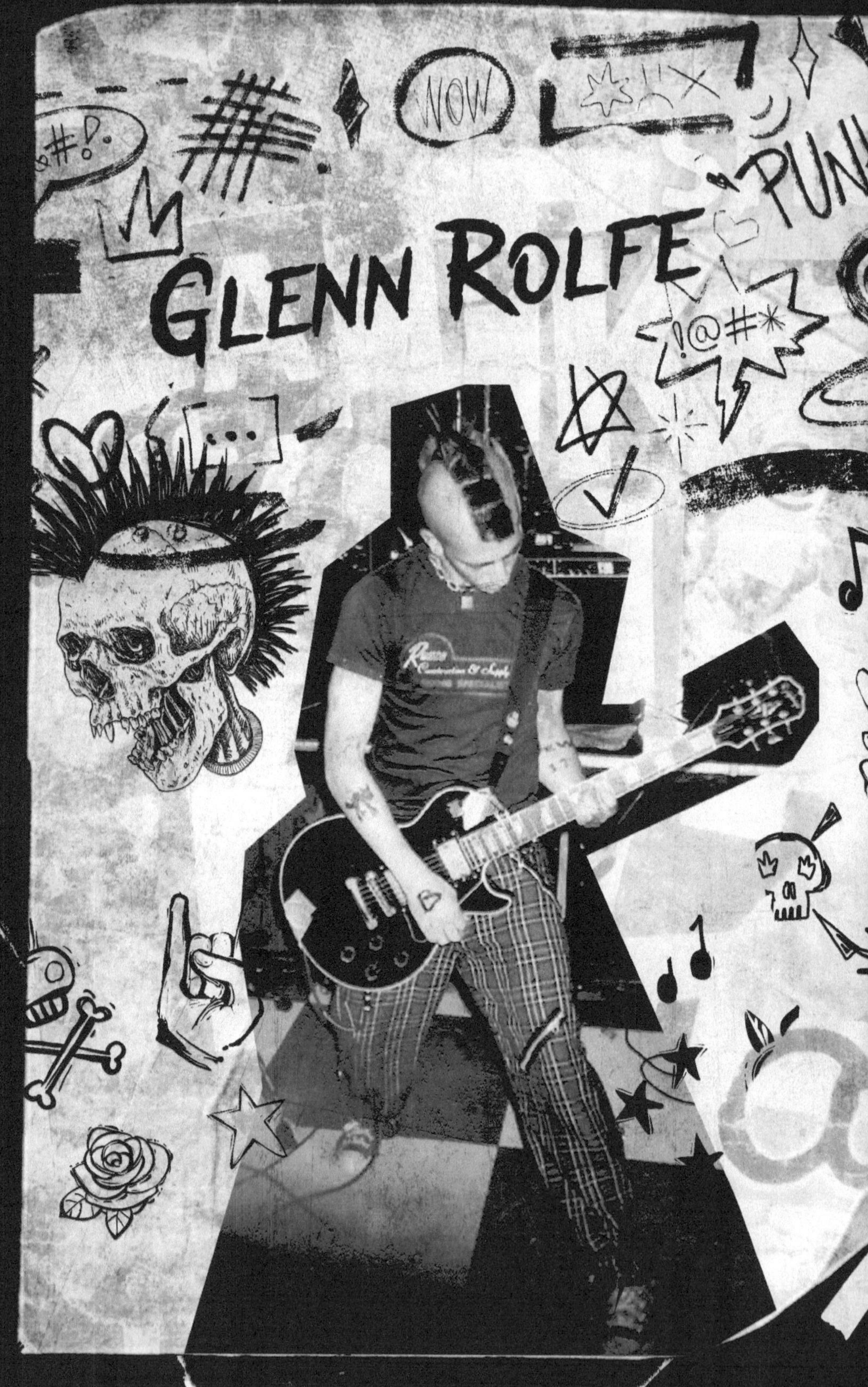

NOW
GLENN ROLFE
PUNK

PULLING TEETH

Glenn Rolfe

Daniel arrived at the VFW hall to see a local punk band called Borderlines. Five bands for the five-dollar cover charge was a good deal. This was his third show in as many weeks. Going to these little punk rock shows had opened a whole new world to him, and he was loving the feeling of community and rebellion—not that he was a rebel, or even part of the community. Daniel was new to the scene. A cassette of All the Stuff and More Vol. 2, by the Ramones, had served as his introduction to punk rock. He went from "Cretin Hop" to "I Just Want to have Something to Do," and every song struck a nerve he didn't even know he had. But one song stood out more than the rest. A melancholy tune called "Questioningly," hit harder than those sped up pop punk tracks. The opening line was striking the perfect chord as he laid eyes upon her.

She was dressed in combat boots and a black 'Screeching Weasel' t-shirt, with orange and black striped stockings beneath a blue plaid skirt. Daniel was a total freak show around girls. His hands got sweaty, a desert storm attacked his throat, and his tongue may as well have been chopped off. He couldn't talk or think straight around a single one of them.

But this particular punk rock girl plopped into his lap. She smiled at him, and he totally froze. Her blonde hair was pulled into pigtails and her blue eyes leveled him. He tried to apologize for standing there, slack jawed, but his mouth couldn't form the words. She kissed his cheek, hopped back to her feet, and rejoined the kids who were thrashing in front of the lone hardcore act on the bill.

For the rest of the show, Daniel was a wallflower stuck in a daze, watching as the girl danced in and out of his sight.

He felt like he was Michael, and she was Star, from The Lost Boys. Or, at least, he wished that could be them.

After the headlining band finished, and despite his fascination with the girl, Daniel tried to slink out the exit unnoticed.

But she was waiting for him, cigarette in hand.

"Sadie" she said, offering him a drag.

"Daniel," he managed. "I don't smoke."

"That's cool. Come on, Danny Boy."

"Where?"

She took him by the hand. "This way."

He tried to resist, albeit not very hard, but Sadie kissed his cheek again and he was under her spell.

They strolled away from the VFW hall under a light sprinkle. It wasn't cold out just yet, but it wasn't warm anymore, either. A light fog accompanied them through the streets.

She smelled like cigarettes and sweat. Normally, Daniel would have found it gross, but something about Sadie made it hit different. Maybe it was some kind of pheromone like Mr. Gillis talked about in Biology. Maybe it was something else. The explanation didn't matter.

He hoped his hands weren't too clammy.

If they were, Sadie kept her revulsion to herself.

"So, Daniel," she said. "What's it like in your world?"

What kind of a question is that?

A Sadie *kind of question,* he answered himself.

"I don't know. I guess I'm still trying to figure it out." He was amazed at how easy the words came. "How...old are you?"

"Seventeen and strung out on confusion," she said. "And you?"

"I'm fifteen. I'm gonna be sixteen in two months."

Shit. I shoulda lied.

"So, "Sadie said. "I'm guessing this will be your first time at a girl's apartment?"

"Wait," he said. "You have your own place?"

"Yep."

She didn't say how or why. Daniel didn't really care.

"Here we are, Danny Boy," she said. "Home sweet home. Come on."

The apartment building was a crummy white three-story structure that looked as if it should be condemned. A number of faded black shutters were missing from the street facing windows. Two of those windows were boarded. The sagging porches on the side of the building were even scarier, and the covered stairways leading to outside entrances for each apartment sagged and appeared rotted in places. Daniel hoped she didn't live on the top floor, and was relieved when she stopped at the door to Apartment #1.

He hesitated.

There was a strange scent, like rotten apples.

"Don't be shy, Daniel, come in."

Sadie smiled, and Daniel followed.

The room was dimly lit by a small lamp in the far corner. Sadie didn't have much furniture. There was only a ratty green sofa that looked like it had been dragged up from the side of the road, a big wooden spool set on its side, and two red milk crates, for chairs, he presumed.

No TV.

She had a few flyers from local punk shows taped on the walls, but it was the series of strange spiraling circles painted in the free space between them that intrigued him.

"Take your coat off," she said. "I won't bite."

Daniel shook out of his green army coat and, checking to make sure there wasn't anything crawling on the fabric—there wasn't—, he set the jacket over the arm of the sofa. He didn't think Sadie looked like she had scabies or bed bugs, but the condition of the couch stirred his anxiety.

She stood in front of the refrigerator in the small kitchen just off the living room. "Do you want a beer?"

"Um…"

"Just kidding."

He let out a nervous laugh and felt like an idiot.

She closed the refrigerator door, opened the freezer, and pulled out a one-liter bottle of clear liquid.

"I only drink vodka."

She took a huge swig from the bottle and walked to Daniel's side, holding it out for him.

He'd never drank in his life.

"For me?" she asked, batting those gorgeous blue eyes.

Daniel took the bottle and tilted it back. He nearly spewed the mouthful of alcohol back out on her.

"It's okay, Danny Boy," Sadie said. "It takes a little getting used to. Go on, try again."

He didn't want to look like a wimp, so he took a big pull from the bottle, trying to shoot the venomous liquid straight to the back of his throat so that he didn't have to taste it.

He couldn't imagine that drinking gasoline would be much different. His throat burned, and it felt like his stomach was sending an intruder alert to his brain. Still, he managed to keep it down.

"Bad ass, huh?" Sadie said.

"Yeah," he lied. "That's good stuff."

She took the bottle, grabbed his hand, and led him over to the sofa.

Sadie took another swig and invited Daniel to do the same, so he did.

"You're quiet," she said, scootching closer to him.

His cheeks warmed, whether from the booze or from Sadie entering his orbit, he wasn't sure.

He ducked his head.

Sadie placed a finger under his chin and brought his face up to meet hers.

His mouth went dry.

She leaned in slow, her mouth inching closer and closer to his, a world of impossibilities crashing like stars into his planet. The world stood still as her lips met his. Sadie's tongue passed his teeth and swirled around his own. For a moment, Daniel thought his brains would turn to mush and drip out of his ears.

She broke the kiss, and Daniel felt like he'd left Earth.

Sadie whispered in his ear. "Give me a minute, and then come down the hall, okay? I've got something really cool to show you."

He swallowed hard. "Sure."

She left the vodka on the floor at his feet.

"Help yourself," she said. "It'll loosen you up."

She stood, walked by him, and disappeared down the hallway without turning on the light. The darkness seemed to swallow her whole.

Daniel thought the vodka was making him swoon like a lovestruck

Romeo, but it could have just as easily been Sadie. He wasn't sure what she had planned, but the thought of getting laid for the first time crossed his dizzy mind. Daniel braved the demon alcohol and took two more swigs from the bottle.

This night was crazy, and it felt dangerous, but after being stuck in his room nearly every Saturday night of his teenage life so far, he wasn't about to waste this chance. Thank goodness for punk rock dragging him out of his shell.

"Daniel?" Sadie called from the dark.

He stood; vodka clutched in his hand. The room swayed. The pulse in his neck pounded a primal beat against his flesh.

He took one more drink and set the bottle down.

"Yeah?" he replied.

"Come on down."

He stumbled to the entry to the hallway.

Holy shit. Am I drunk?

He felt the wall for a light switch and found the little plastic nub.

He tried flicking it, but nothing happened.

"Sadie?"

Silence.

Daniel stepped into the corridor.

The rotten apple smell grew stronger. As he moved further into the hall, he noticed a pungent, sour milk scent buried beneath the others. His stomach lurched. Daniel covered his nose and stopped. The light from the living room died, leaving him in total blackness.

Daniel spun and held the wall to steady himself.

Something heavy thudded at the end of the corridor.

"Sadie?"

A soft light danced to life beneath a closed door further down the hall.

Daniel wanted to run, but he was too dizzy. Instead, he made his way towards Sadie, towards the door with the flickering light, towards oblivion.

"Come in, Daniel."

He reached out nudged the door with his fingertips.

The creak of the opening door raised the hairs on the back of Daniel's neck, but his body's intuitive warning did nothing to prepare him for the horrors held within the nauseating room.

Human remains filled the room in varying degrees of fester and decay, all surrounding an empty, waiting, hospital bed. Daniel's knees went weak as his stomach betrayed him. Vomit ripped up from his guts, violating his esophagus, and exploding from his mouth. He dropped to his knees, heaving up more and more bile as his eyes continued to take in the macabre sights of this place. Viscous puddles caressed putrid remains—limbs, ruined organs, and rotten flesh, faces without skin, and clumps of hair and bone were all set pell-mell around the room.

Daniel was certain this was some fever dream nightmare.

This was the cave of a fictional monster; a demonic entity sent to devour and devastate human beings. To untether them from their souls.

He dropped his chin and dry heaved several more times, stomach empty but searching for more.

Sadie. Where is Sadie?

He raised his head in time to see the club hammer swing before him. It smashed into his mouth.

His front teeth shattered, their deeper roots twisting and ruining the gums that had held them in place for years. Blood flowed like a crimson river down his lips and over his tongue as he flopped backwards and collapsed. Pain overrode Daniel's sense of fear and survival, leaving him crying and convulsing in the doorway. He choked on his own blood as he felt himself get dragged into the horror room.

Sadie growled and grunted as she hefted him off the floor and over her shoulder. Daniel gurgled through his broken mouth and grasped at her pigtails.

She thwarted his pathetic attempts to stop her and shrugged his body onto the hospital bed. She disappeared as he spat blood and teeth and tried to breathe. Daniel lifted his head as she propped herself up in front of him and feigned another swing with the hammer.

Daniel turned his head to the side.

He cried, readying himself for another strike that never came.

Instead, something dropped across his thighs. Pulled itself taut.

A second strap dropped across his chest and tightened as well.

Daniel tried to beg, but his ruined mouth could no longer make the words.

"Don't move," Sadie said with a smile, bending over and kissing his forehead. "I'll be right back."

Daniel had gone to the show alone. He'd just told his parents he was going to the VFW hall and that he'd be back late, and they had trusted him. They wouldn't bother waiting up, they'd just go to bed. His parents wouldn't even know he was missing. Not tonight. Not while he was still... alive. Nobody knew he was here, strapped to a bed, struggling not to choke on his own blood, and surrounded by death in a creepy apartment building—

Oh God, where are we? I didn't even pay attention to where she brought me. I don't know what street I'm on.

Whatever effect the vodka had on him earlier seemed to have been jettisoned by Sadie's brutal attack. Splashed out, along with the rest of his stomach's contents, across the bedroom floor. Part of him wished he could finish the bottle. To not have to feel this pain a second longer. To not have to be consumed by the mistake, the terrible, stupid choices he'd made that put him right here, right now.

He needed to get out of these straps. Daniel needed to look for an exit, but he didn't want to see the body parts around him. The visions of what this beautiful girl had done to these people. How could she—

"Aw, Daniel," Sadie said entering the room. "You waited for me."

Daniel groaned, but still couldn't say anything intelligible.

"I waited for you, too. Now, let's have some real fun."

Daniel saw the handsaw in Sadie's hand. His eyes went wide. He struggled against his bindings.

Without a word, Sadie dragged the blood-stained saw across his shins.

Daniel screamed.

She did it again.

Blood, Daniel's blood, splattered across her skirt and stockings. Each tiny sawblade tore through his skin and cut to the bone. Daniel's mind summersaulted as he felt the individual teeth of the jagged saw scrape and jerk with unbound violence over his shin bones. Sadie worked the simple tool back and forth, grinning, her blue eyes glazed over with a sadistic glee that Daniel wished he'd noticed before.

Daniel wailed.

Someone's got to hear me.

Someone has to save me.

Sadie stood on her toes and thrust the blade forward with all of her weight. The saw ripped through the side of Daniel's right calf muscle, sending chunks of flesh and muscular tissue to the floor, to land with a series of sickening plops.

Daniel's screech filled the room with a symphony of suffering.

He mewled and spasmed, his head thrashing the slim pillow beneath his skull as Sadie pivoted the blade, crouched and dragged the saw toward her. Daniel's left calf muscle frayed, showering her skirt and tights with more of the viscous pulp.

Sadie stayed crouched for a moment, catching her breath. She wiped her blood-spattered forearm across her sweaty brow and reveled in the copious amount of blood and gore.

Her heartbeat steadied. She took in a deep breath and rose, ready for the next round.

"Do you want to know why I waited for you, Daniel? Hmm?"

Sadie lightly set the blood-drenched teeth of the saw against his stomach.

Daniel flopped like a fish.

"I have a gift," Sadie said, using the tip of the saw to raise the bottom of his t-shirt, exposing the soft flesh of his stomach. "It's normal to resist. They all do. We just don't realize how truly trapped we all are."

She grinned as Daniel's stomach muscles tensed.

"But," she continued. "We get a dose of truth when the pain comes."

She leaned in and hauled the saw across his stomach.

He cried out. A wave of lightheadedness arrived like an empty promise. Passing out would have assure his death, but Daniel had never wanted to meet extinction so bad in his life.

"You feel that?" Sadie asked. "Go to it, that freeing sensation. It's a portal. It's the way out."

He barely heard her bizarre rhetoric. She may as well have been speaking in another language, one only understood by the insane.

"Those are some nasty cuts, Daniel. I'd let go sooner than later if I were you."

Daniel wanted nothing more. He didn't want to feel any of it anymore.

Sadie tossed the handsaw to the floor, bent down, and came up with the club hammer again.

"You're gonna be all busted up."

She spoke sweetly, her eyes suddenly soft and vulnerable as she brushed the bloody hand without the hammer through his hair. "I think I love you, Daniel. So pretty please, for me, just let go."

Sadie kissed his forehead, walked back down to his legs and raised the hammer.

He screamed again.

The hammer smashed into his left knee. The frenzied, melodic bliss of Daniel's cries danced in perfect step with the crack, crunch, and pop of pulverized bones and snapping ligaments.

His screams continued as Sadie walked around and delivered the same devastation to his right knee.

The wooziness returned, lifting him with immense speed up, up, up…

"Yes, Daniel," he heard Sadie's voice as if she were in another room. "There it is, Daniel. You're free."

And he was.

Gone.

Into the void.

Blackness.

Total darkness.

* * *

Daniel opened his eyes.

The room was full of sunlight and music.

Jesse Michaels was singing about a smiling when your friends were watching you.

Daniel's mouth was dry, but his pain was...gone.

He forced his head up and looked down at his wounds. He was shirtless, and his stomach was bandaged up. His legs were hidden under a big blue blanket.

There was a tray on a stack of milk crates next to his bed.

A bottle of water and a couple slice of bread.

The door across the room opened.

"You're awake," Said hurried to his side.

Daniel instinctively recoiled.

"I know, I know," she said. "You shouldn't be here, but I just couldn't let you go. Not yet. I love you, Daniel. I think I'm going to keep you around a while longer."

"My..." he said, his voice scratchy. "My parents will call the cops. They'll find me."

"Oh, Daniel," she walked to the door. "They'll look, but we left my apartment three days ago, silly. Look out that window. Don't you recognize the California sun when you see it?"

California?

"Listen," she said. "You need your rest. I can't keep you for long. That's not what I do. Once you're healed up enough, we'll have to do it all over again, okay. I love you."

He couldn't speak.

Again?

Sadie's eyebrows knitted together. "Daniel, don't you have something to say?"

You're fucking crazy!

You're fucking disturbed!

"Do I need to go get my saw?" she asked.

"No," he managed. "No."

"So, say it."

Daniel swallowed hard. "I love you, too."

"You are just the sweetest boy."

She stepped out and closed the door.

Tears welled up in Daniel's eyes.

What had she meant, *we'll have to do it all over again?*

'PUNK'
#MAX BOOTH III
GHOULISH BOOKS
GHOULISH BOOTH

KIDS OF THE BLACK HOLE

Max Booth III

You don't find out about the black hole until a month after you've moved into the house. It's in the basement, wrapped in an itchy military blanket someone scavenged from a dumpster ages before you showed up at Smegma Haus, begging to be taken in—left eye swollen and bruised, lip split, dried blood still flaking out of your nostrils, the last words of your dad still ringing in your ears like tinnitus: *You wanna be a boy so much, then I'm gonna punish you like one.* It's been weeks since you've seen him, and still, you wonder if those fists raining down upon your face had been his way of accepting or rejecting your identity.

In a sick, fucked-up epiphany, it warms your heart to believe he would've never punched a girl.

You keep telling yourself that until it feels true.

Scab's the one who brings the black hole up. "You haven't seen it yet?" they ask, giggling. "Shit, kid, you *gotta* see the black hole. It's gonna blow your mind, kid."

You hate the way they call you *kid.* A reminder that you're the youngest current resident of Smegma Haus. That it was a whole debate initially, whether the community should allow you to move in or kick your ass to the curb.

What are we, a fuckin' daycare now? someone had asked, and you'd sucked in the urge to cry and tried to defend yourself, told them you weren't that young. *I'm almost fourteen,* you had tried to say, but couldn't find the breath to speak, full panic attack absorbing you until someone grabbed your hand and led you to a safe, quiet room to calm down. You'd overheard a bunch of them bickering outside the door, how it went against the ethics of the house to turn away someone in need, that they had all been that young once, and wouldn't they'd all have been better off somewhere like here, instead of the shit-ass families from their upbringings?

"What black hole?" you ask, feeling like you're the brunt of some inside joke. "You mean like in space?"

Everybody's sitting around the furniture-less living room, blasting Bad Brains and getting wasted. Everybody except for you, it seems.

Beer still scares you.

You've seen what it does to your dad. You never want to touch the stuff for as long as you live. A variety of drugs move around the mass of sweaty teenage bodies, too, but drugs terrify you way more than beer. Especially after what happened with your mom when you were younger. You try to work up the courage to take a puff of something, to make an attempt to *belong* and to prove you're one of their peers and not some *kid* who needs to be babysat. But the fear of overdosing is strong enough to keep you paralyzed on the roach-infested carpet with your hands folded in your lap.

Maybe they won't notice how much of a square you really are.

Maybe they'll forget that you don't belong here.

"Well shit, kid," Scab says, over the music which never seems to die down no matter the hour, "it *could've* come from space. Truth is, kid, we don't really know." They turn to everybody else, and they ask, "Do we?"

And they all shake their heads, still giggling, in possession of privileged knowledge. Then, because nobody in Smegma Haus is infamous for their patience, everybody collects their flashlights and leads you to the basement.

A bizarre noise creeps into your ears the moment you reach the top step, and it only intensifies the deeper into the basement you plunge. The harder you focus on it, the harder it is to understand. Something kind of like microwave static, an inexplicable chittering nonsense. Nobody else seems to acknowledge it, so you decide it must be in your head.

The whole way down, you're thinking this is a prank, that they're setting you up for some kind of practical joke. That—or something much meaner. They've realized their mistake in letting you stay here, and today's the day they finalize your eviction. They're going to beat the shit out of you and then they'll drag your weeping body to the street. The idea seems so probable that it's a struggle not to burst into tears. The anticipation of rejection makes you want to vomit. The only thing holding you back is the lack of anything in your stomach. All you've been eating lately is handfuls of dry cereal.

But nobody here beats the shit out of you.

At least, not yet.

Instead, Scab and someone else approach an item concealed by that military blanket—the one you've spotted before, on the few occasions when you've been brave enough to come down here. You once asked another kid—one not much older than yourself—if you could claim the blanket for your sleeping area upstairs, and she'd looked at you like you were out of your mind.

Never go near that blanket, she'd said, dead-serious, and you'd listened.

At least, until now you had.

You don't know what you're expecting to find under the blanket, but a box isn't it.

A large metal trunk. Midnight black.

A person could fit inside if they were limber enough. It'd be tight, but they could fit.

You're struck with the absolute certainty that the members of Smegma Haus are going to cram you inside it as a joke. That they're going to take turns sitting on the lid, listening to you punch and kick and scream until all of the oxygen drains from your lungs. *Turn around,* you think. *Run far away—before it's too late.*

But the truth is, there's nowhere else for you to go. You can't return home. Maybe if you'd only been gone a day or two, but a *month*? You wouldn't be able to live with yourself. Smegma Haus is your home now. At least, it is until a better opportunity arises.

A better opportunity like the inside of a mysterious box hidden in the basement of an abandoned house?

"What's in there?" you ask, terrified to find out.

"I already told you, kid," Scab says, smirking.

A black hole.

Then they undo the latches and swing the lid open.

Too late, you realize everybody else has already pulled the fronts of their shirts up over their noses—or, at least, the kids who are *wearing* shirts do. There's a lot of Smegma Haus residents—of any and all genders—who prefer to go around topless during the day, until the cold of the night kicks in.

You, personally, can't imagine ever having the courage to take your shirt off in front of someone. Not even you can stand the sight of your chest. The duct tape helps *somewhat*, even if it makes it hard to breathe and hurts like a motherfucker whenever you change it out. But that only works with a shirt still draped over your torso. Although it *does* get hot here—*really* fucking hot, actually—which only further complicates the tape the more you sweat. The house doesn't have any power, which means no heat and no air conditioning. No *anything*, really, except for the freedom of existing.

The shirtless ones have squeezed their nostrils together with their fingers, but the smell hits you full-force—so strong, you're again grateful to be down here on an empty stomach.

Rot is the first word that comes to mind.

Decay.

Something in this box has died.

Something *awful.*

What you're smelling is death.

But you don't run away.

Instead, you inch closer…

Close enough that you can glimpse inside, your flashlight shining directly into the box's unhinged maw, revealing a darkness.

Not *nothing.*

A blackness.

Thick like syrup.

Pulsating, you think.

It's alive.

And you have to bite back the question you want to ask—*what is this?*—because you already know how Scab will answer.

I told you, kid. It's a black hole.

The second question you have—*is it safe*—sounds too much like a baby's concern, so you ask the next logical thing that comes to mind:

"What does it do?"

You know it does *something,* otherwise it wouldn't be hidden down here—out of view, protected. Whatever this is, it's special, and you can't look away from it. Even the smell isn't that bad after a few minutes. Not like the others are reacting. You adjust to it quickly. You start to welcome it.

"It eats," Scab replies, and everybody's laughing again. "You wanna see it feed, kid?"

You nod without saying anything. All paranoia of Smegma Haus betraying you vanishes. These other kids wouldn't have shown you something like this if they were planning on exiling you from the premises.

You're one of them.

Maybe not a *family*, but certainly linked together.

Bonded.

Hell yeah you want to see this weird box eat something.

Of *course* you do.

Stella—this older girl with a fading pink mohawk—runs upstairs to collect something in the back yard, then returns with a long branch she's snapped off one of the trees surrounding Smegma Haus. She hands it to you like she's presenting a delicate gift, and you accept it, feeling deeply honored.

"What do I do?" you ask the basement, but you already know the answer.

Feed it.

The stick's far longer than the perceived depth of the box, but something tells you that won't be an issue. To test it, you raise the stick over the opening and slowly lower it into the thick blackness pulsating inside. The dark nothing latches onto the wood, allowing the rest of the branch to smoothly enter its enchanting void. Eventually, you're left with no choice but to release your grip and let the remaining bit of it drop down and vanish.

To be swallowed.

It never crosses your mind that there might be a trick floor beneath the box. Nothing about what you've just witnessed screams *illusion*. Whatever this is, it's real. It's the realest thing you've ever known.

"What else have you put inside it?" you ask, and now it's time for another round of shared laughter in the basement.

"Oh man, so much shit," Scab says. "It's mostly what we do around here, when we can't think of anything else to pass the time." Then they list some of the items Smegma Haus residents have fed to the box over the years: sticks, yes, but also rocks, stop signs, firecrackers, empty beer cans, mail stolen from the neighbors, pretty much anything they could think of, they'd tried. The only line they'd really drawn was at anything living. So, no animals—outside of roadkill, which didn't count since those animals were already dead, anyway.

"Do you know where it goes?"

"Not a fuckin' clue," Scab says. "What happens when *anything* falls into a black hole, right?"

"Spaghettification," someone says in the back of the basement. "Assuming, uh, it's a real black hole—ya know, like a real scientific one, and not…uh, something else."

You don't have to ask what *spaghettification* means. It sounds perfectly self-explanatory.

"What else could it be?" you ask next. Then, because the question's been on the tip of your tongue since they opened the trunk: "Where did you get it?"

"Shit, kid, *I* didn't get nothin'. This thing was here long before I ever moved in." Scab glances down at the box, grimaces, and kicks the lid shut. "Sorry, after so long that smell starts giving me a migraine."

A few of the others add that their heads are also hurting, and they're relieved Scab's finally closed it. You don't let them know that you're feeling fine.

More than fine, even.

This is the best you've ever felt in your life, maybe.

"I first came to Smegma Haus three years ago," Scab continues. "Back then, this guy named Louie was kinda the person in charge. Not that anybody's actually *in charge.* He just mentored a lot of people, you know what I mean, kid? Pulled more than his fair share of weight. Kind of a fuckin' inspiration, if you wanna know the truth."

"Aw," Stella says, "I miss Louie."

"What happened to him?" you ask, afraid the answer's going to involve Louie falling into the box and disappearing.

"The worst possible thing you could ever imagine," Scab says. "He got an office job downtown and started a nuclear family."

Everybody in the basement makes a sound of disgust. You mimic one seconds after, still trying your best to fit in.

"But anyway," Scab says, "before he became a poser, he was pretty rad. He introduced me to the black hole down here. Told me it was here to protect us, and we were here to protect *it*. But this thing was here even before *he* moved in. It's hard to trace back how long, exactly, this box has been in this basement. Maybe before it even became a punk house. Shit, the original residents could have brought it here, whoever the hell they were. How am I supposed to know, kid?"

Scab lights a joint, then passes it to you. Everybody's watching. Every eye is on this moment. You accept it and take a drag and your chest bursts into flames and suddenly you can't stop coughing, it burns so goddamn much, which everybody thinks is the most hysterical thing in the world. You take another drag, just to show you're not a pussy, then pass it on to the closest person to you. You don't feel anything besides the burning in your chest and throat and nose. Maybe you didn't do it right. Or maybe you're overdosing like you feared. All you can think about now is your mom and you're trying so hard not to cry in front of everybody.

"I heard a story once," Scab says. "Something that was passed on to Louie, which he passed on to me, which I've passed on to all of you at one time or another—and now I'll do the same for *you*, too, kid."

"What kind of story?" you ask, hyper focused on the beam emitting from your flashlight.

"About how the black hole got created," Scab says, then shines their own flashlight under their jaw, real spooky campfire story vibes. "The way I heard it, years and years ago, before any of us were even born, before this house was even built maybe, these kids caught a monster in the woods."

"A monster? What kind of monster?"

Scab shrugs. "I don't know. Just a monster. Use your imagination, okay?"

You try to imagine a monster and all you see is your dad.

"Anyway, these kids find this monster, right? And they fuckin'...trap it somehow. They fuckin' *torture* this thing, you know? Real evil shit. Burning it with cigarettes, breaking its fingers, any cruel thing you can imagine, they probably did some form of it. And they keep this monster for days and days, making it experience all sorts of pain—and then, once they're tired of it, they stuff its body in some box—*this* box. And they lock it so the monster can't escape, and they dig a big hole in the woods and bury it out there. They leave it to die, alone and forgotten. And once it *does* die, it begins decomposing. But this is a monster we're talking about here. Not an animal, or whatever. A fuckin' *monster*. And monsters, man, monsters rot different than humans. Their corpses evolve in ways we can't even begin to understand. That's why it reeks of something decomposing—because it *is* decomposing. You understand what I'm saying, kid?"

"So, the black hole is just a monster that died a long time ago?" you ask, feeling like you're standing on a cloud. Everything is floating, everything is soft.

You take another drag of the joint and pass it onward.

This time you don't cough.

This time it feels *good*.

Again, Scab shrugs. "No fucking idea, kid. Maybe Louie was just high and thought it'd be funny to screw with me. Or maybe the person who told Louie had been trying to screw with *him*. How do you even begin to fact check when it comes to shit like this?"

Then you ask one final question, perhaps the most important one you've wanted answered since looking inside.

"Has anyone ever tried sticking part of themselves into it? Like, their hand, or something?"

And the way Scab stares at you, the answer is already obvious.

"No," they say, "holy shit, no, why would anyone do that?"

"Just to see how it feels, I guess," you try to explain, feeling self-conscious.

You thought for sure the others would have wondered the same thing.

How could they *not*, right?

It's all you've been thinking about.

"I don't think anyone's done that. It wouldn't be a good idea. We don't know what would happen. What if it bit off your hand? Or, shit, what if it sucked the rest of you through, like some gnarly vacuum cleaner?" Scab glances down at the joint in their hand, then extinguishes it with the knee of their jeans. "I think maybe that's enough black hole shenanigans for one day."

You follow everybody back upstairs without protesting. Everybody else seems in agreeance.

The party's over.

Ruined, maybe, by your own curiosity.

You don't even mention how there could be easy ways to test something like that before sticking your own hand through. For instance, the black hole hadn't bit through the stick you inserted earlier. You're pretty sure you could have pulled it back out if you had wanted to—before letting it get completely swallowed.

It's weird how quickly Scab shot down your question. Almost like it was a lie. Like someone *has* tried your idea before—and, for whatever reason, they do not want you to find out what'd happened. Which in itself is *weird*, right? Because why show you the black hole at all if there's secrets they want to keep about it? Why hide *anything* at this point?

That night, you can't sleep. Your brain feels like a pinball machine going apeshit. All you can think about is what's below you. How it's waiting for you, practically begging you to open it again. As fucked up as it sounds, you even miss the smell.

Eventually, you have to pee. Miraculously, Smegma Haus has an active water supply. Someone tampered with the meter in the back yard, apparently, and nobody from the city's ever come out to investigate.

Like every room here, the bathroom is a disaster, but the toilet works and that's all you can ask for in times like these.

Would you rather be back at your dad's house?

Highly fucking doubtful.

Another thing about Smegma Haus is it's never silent. There's always music of some type blaring at a neighborhood-disturbing level of volume. Sometimes it gives you a headache and you wish they'd turn it down—just for a little bit, so you can calm your thoughts and hear yourself think.

But tonight, the music is a blessing.

It means nobody hears you creep back down to the basement.

The basement, which you think might be off-limits without Scab's supervision, even if Smegma Haus technically doesn't have any rules.

You suspect this might be one of those *unspoken* ones.

You also don't give a shit about breaking it.

If you wanted to follow someone else's rules, you wouldn't be here in the first place.

The box opens easily enough. It's unlocked, which feels like a mistake. Something this unique needs to be better guarded. Anybody could come down here and mess with it. Maybe you'll start living down here, after all. There's a lot of room. Plenty of space to breathe, to think.

The smell of decay makes everything feel disorienting, but not in an unpleasant way. You wonder if you're still high from earlier. Your legs start trembling, turning to rubber, and you fall to your knees, hands clutching the edge of the box as you look straight down into the infinite blackness greeting you inside.

You can't see a goddamn thing down here. Your flashlight is still upstairs, next to the pile of beach towels you use for a pillow.

Not that you need it.

Light isn't necessary for something like this.

Instead, it's better to accept the nothingness—to embrace the void.

And that's just what you do.

Except…you don't bother sticking your hand inside.

If you're going to commit, then you're going to fucking commit.

So you plunge your face forward, almost like you're bobbing for apples.

Toward the smell of decay.

Toward the subtle, unintelligible chittering you've been hearing since Scab first opened the box.

The chittering that's been beckoning to you—calling you by name.

By your *true* name.

The one you've gifted yourself.

The sensation is overwhelming as you dunk your face into the black hole. So cold, so goddamn intoxicatingly cold. It's like diving into a lake in early spring, and your first instinct is to pull away, to go back upstairs, but there's no retreating at this point. You physically can't bring yourself to do it. Whatever spell this is, it's locked in nice and tight. You are here to stay.

At least until you've seen what it is that the black hole wants you to see.

Which, it turns out, is everything.

The black hole shows you everything.

Everything that once was, and ever will be.

Within the blink of an eye, the entire history of the universe—past, present, and future—injects itself into your brain.

You see yourself being born.

You see your mom overdosing on sleeping pills.

You see your dad sobbing on the couch, surrounded by empty cans of beer.

You see yourself finding yourself.

You see your dad finally tracking you down to Smegma Haus.

You see the fight that ensues.

You see how it ends, with his neck snapping against the bottom step to this very basement.

You see Scab and the others helping you stuff your dad's body into the box, disappearing his corpse into the black hole, all of you vowing to never speak of the incident again.

You see them all pitching in to give you some going-away money. You can't stay here now. Not after what happened. You have to keep moving. You have to escape.

You see yourself hopping on a passing train.

You see strangers trying to harm you, some of them failing, so many of them succeeding.

You see yourself surviving, again and again and again.

You see yourself becoming a man, the kind of man you always dreamed of becoming, the kind of man you always were.

You see yourself growing old.

You see yourself getting sick.

You see the planet rotting.

You see genocide and atrocity and so, so much death.

You see it all.

The good things, the bad things, the wonderful things, the nightmarish things.

For better or worse, all of these things are inside you now.

Whenever you close your eyes, you will see them.

Whenever you open your eyes, they will still be there—*waiting*.

There is nothing you will be able to do to stop any of it. It's already happened. Just because you're here now in this basement doesn't mean you aren't everywhere else you've ever been or ever will be, either.

It is all happening now, right fucking now.

You see everything and it's all so incredible and it's all so ugly and it's all so goddamn beautiful you swear you could cry.

But you don't.

You don't dare give this box a single tear.

All your life, others have tried writing your future, telling you who you were, telling you who you weren't.

Like you never had a choice, like none of this shit was ever up to you.

But fuck that.

And fuck this box.

You'll carve out your own destiny from the carcasses of any miserable bastard who dares to get in your way.

When the black hole finally regurgitates your face out of its magic rot, you offer it the only appropriate gift that comes to mind.

A thick, juicy loogie directly into its predictable void.

Then you slam the box shut and go back upstairs to start packing.

Your time at Smegma Haus has come to an end.

WOW
STAY HELLBEN
SAMO
HELLBENT
FOR
HORROR

LET'S LYNCH THE LANDLORD

S.A. Bradley

A fleet of food trucks smashed through the entrance to Berkeley's downtown Police Department, spewing tacos, hot dogs, and condiments as they disappeared through the gaping hole they'd created; the spot where sliding glass doors and metal detectors had used to be.

Who would have thought there would be take-out during the apocalypse?

Black smoke billowed out of the station as, somewhere deep inside, a propane tank ruptured and, I gotta admit, this is some extreme shit for a Thursday morning. Even for this town.

My campsite is high in the Berkeley hills, nestled beneath the Lawrence Hall of Science's observation deck. Until recently, first-year students had brought their upper-middle-class parents here to take in the panoramic view that was almost as heart-stopping as their yearly tuition costs. If those parents knew that this guy, living out of an old sleeping bag, held the same master's degree in Nuclear Engineering that their kids were pursuing, they'd probably have thrown themselves off the edge.

It's been nearly 50 years since I graduated, and it's been almost 40 years since I emancipated myself from the bullshit and went off the grid.

Berkeley was different back then.

I hardly recognize it now.

However, from my vantage point, I can see the smoldering remains of the University Chancellor's mansion, a crumbling City Hall, several immolating police stations, and I have to say… things are looking up.

Listen. This DIY system correction has been coming for a long time. It's no secret that the tech bros, LLCs, and corporate landlords bought up entire neighborhoods in San Francisco and pushed out family businesses to make more cash. They gobbled up warehouses and sent artists and advocates packing, priced out working families, and gentrified downtown to cater to the select few. Landlords became as rich as dukes.

And when it was just happening in San Fransisco, the punks had abided it.

But those greedy fuckers decided to bring their rigged game to Oakland; to my United Republic of Berkeley. And so, they met the biggest, baddest landlord baron of them all. You might believe UC Berkeley's reputation as the liberal capital of the world, but that just describes our students and our faculty. The *institution* was all about money. Land. And that machine was ruthless in collecting both. The institution tolerated radical campus behavior until it cost them their favorite things.

The University, the tech bros, and the Berkeley police all joined forces to "beautify their town." To "make it safer for everyone." To "improve public health."

That was all code for "get rid of these homeless encampments because they're making donors nervous."

Let me tell you, when you live outdoors, "beautification" is an ugly business.

Not gonna lie, those pricks succeeded in pushing folks into dark holes for a long time.

But they got power drunk and greedy, like bullies do. And the way things look right now? It seems like the East Bay finally had enough of their bullshit.

The countdown to the apocalypse started when the Chancellor decided to settle an old score over a very public thorn in the University's side: People's Park, an infamous parcel of land, just slightly under three acres in size, but with an oversized reputation. A defiant, scuzzy monument to "Fuck you; I won't do what you say." I used to be a "Parkie," myself. A longstanding resident of People's, before the morons attempted their kill shot. People's Park had been a battlefield from the beginning. It was born from a botched eminent domain land grab by the UC that left it laying abandoned for over a year. Until a handful of activists planted trees and organized a community on the grounds, at which point the Chancellor sent the Berkeley police to beat the shit out of them all.

The cops got more than they expected when 3000 students and residents marched to the park to punch back. Sheriffs in riot gear bashed skulls with nightsticks, but the protestors stood up for themselves and set fire to police cruisers. The angry crowd swelled as more people joined the carnage, and bricks and bottles rained down. The cops had fired fucking *shotguns* into the crowd, and buckshot ripped through nineteen-year-olds and middle-aged neighbors alike. Blood was everywhere. People slipped on crimson puddles in the dirt. Governor Ronald Reagan sent in the National Guard, who dropped tear gas on the city from helicopters. The gas wafted for miles, and sick kids filled the hospitals.

Before "Bloody Thursday" ended, 128 civilians had been hospitalized. James Rector, who watched from the roof of a bookstore, was gunned down in cold blood.

All this over three acres of mud.

It had to have been that blood, man. All the blood shed within the park must have consecrated the ground somehow. Decade after decade, psychically charging the site until it finally... like... erupted.

Or, maybe it was all the "counterculture casualties" like me, the skate punks, and the 5150 psych patients without health care who all claimed sanctuary in the park. Maybe it's because we created a fucked up, de facto community. A home for lost causes. Maybe all those lost causes decided People's Park was as good a place as any to make a last stand and fight back.

Death or glory, motherfuckers.

Fellow parkies like myself, Shopping Cart Gilda, Ace Backwords, Wild Billy Wolff, B.N. Duncan, Hippie Boy, Narayana, Minerva, Vincent

Johnson, Gypsy Catano, and Sparky. We all chose to make our homes in People's Park.

Hate Man, beloved for shouting "I hate you" at passersby, had been an Air Force intelligence officer and a New York Times reporter until he saw the ugly face of the system he supported. Then he'd dropped out. Decided to become, instead, someone the broken street kids could trust. Hate Man wore a goofy, floppy fisherman's cap covered with enamel pins and paper flowers that made him approachable, even to the timid ones. He lined the pockets of his scruffy coat with free smokes, which he offered to newcomers as long as they leaned into him, shoulder-to-shoulder, and tried to push him over.

How had he known they craved physical touch, but could never ask for it?

Hate Man is gone now.

When he was dying, he demanded to get back to the park. He passed away under his tree, marked with an "H."

Like Hate Man, all my friends are gone now.

Like Hate Man, all my friends left their souls in the park.

The beginning of the end happened quickly. The State Supreme Court gave in to the University's demands and handed them the legal right to build student housing on People's Park, just as long as UC Berkeley promised to "include a facility for the unhoused park residents."

Yeah, right.

On the night of the transfer, I heard the spotlights' electric click before the beams landed upon the encampment. When the Chancellor's berserkers arrived, they made as much noise as possible, as if trying to heighten our terror.

Silhouettes in riot gear lined up at the park's edge, smacking their shields with batons, savoring our helplessness.

Unintelligible rules shouted through bullhorns which we had, supposedly, already broken.

The police line marched through our homes at a leisurely pace, swinging batons like scythes harvesting crops. They ripped through tents, shattered plastic lawn chairs, and tore apart backpacks, tossing our meager belongings into the night sky.

Groggy parkies stumbled deeper into the darkness.

Those on crutches struggled to stay ahead of the advancing squad.

A wheelchair-bound woman was stuck in a rut, and she started crying. I grabbed the handles and dragged the chair backwards, aiming for the street. Two cops advanced on us fast, and I realized they'd get to us before we got to the street. Fuck it; I figured I could take a few hits and get this woman to the safety of public streetlights before I went down. I kept my speed and braced for the familiar kiss of steel.

A young, dumb tweaker got between us, stood his ground, and yelled at the troopers. They shot him in the throat with a taser and laughed as he fish-flopped in the dirt.

I heard screams in the dark from those too slow to get out of the way of progress.

A blitzkrieg of bulldozers followed behind the police, devouring everything that got left behind.

The encampment was gone in minutes.

160 double-stacked storage containers surrounded People's Park by the next morning, creating an 18-foot-high perimeter of steel that stretched from Haste and Bowditch to Dwight Way, then down to Telegraph Avenue.

Security guards operated fortified checkpoints.

Spotlights rimmed the top of the structure.

Nobody was gonna sneak into the home of the Free Speech Stage. Not on their watch.

They built the Berlin Wall in Berkeley, and somewhere, Ronald Regan was surely laughing his ass off.

But we weren't going to go quietly.

Fuck going quietly.

The night after the steel wall went up, residents on late-night dog walks reported seeing what looked like a group of skeletons wearing black hoodies and cargo pants, riding skateboards, jumping the steps at Sproul Plaza.

And that's weird, even by Berkely standards. Like, what the fuck, right?

A second bone crew was reportedly seen hopping the turnstiles at the Shattuck BART station, doing aerials and half-pipes into the subway tunnel.

More skeletons were spotted at Oakland's Lake Merritt, stealing a racing boat from the rowing club and paddling into the estuary.

At the time, police departments had assumed the calls were hoaxes.

They don't believe that anymore.

The next morning, I had to show up for the start of the demolition. I couldn't stay away. There was a modest crowd of protestors, most of them the "usual suspects." The same people who'd been protesting shit for decades. But they only showed up for the cameras, so I tuned them out.

Because of the wall of shipping containers, I could only hear what was happening. But I knew the park by memory, so I closed my eyes and followed the sound of the bulldozer's trajectory.

I listened as the green lawn, where hippie chicks danced while we drummed on plastic buckets, got torn from the roots.

I cringed as the wet splatter of community garden vegetables got crushed under the vehicle's treads.

I heard the collapse of the basketball court, where Jerry Rubin and I once played one-on-one to settle a political argument (I won).

The bulldozer moved on and invaded the small grove of trees. I remembered the faces of the people who had planted them fifty years ago as each tree fell, one at a time, executioner-style.

I counted them all as they died, and I held my breath as I realized which tree was next.

The machine revved its strained engine.

The startlingly loud crack of thick, healthy wood yielding to an overwhelming force hit me like a slap. Hate Man's tree, tattooed with an "H," was no more.

Drops of rain fell on my face, and I heard construction workers shouting at each other. When I opened my eyes, I saw a massive plume of water shooting into the sky.

Apparently, Hate Man's tree had taken root around a water main and loosened a pipe. I smiled. I thought that my friend had gotten in one last "I hate you" over on the pricks, but I hadn't known the half of it. Not yet.

Construction was postponed, and the protestors got a short reprieve.

But then, when the sun went down, and the Punks took their turn again.

Across the Golden Gate Bridge, into Marin, park rangers at Mount Tamalpais responded to what they assumed were poachers on one of the fire trails. They set up a roadblock when they saw a line of lights quickly descending the mountain.

Two dozen mountain bikers flew down the steep trail at breakneck speed, riding old 1940s single-speed balloon tire Schwinn bicycles. "Klunkers," like the crazy Larkspur Canyon Gang used to ride. Except these riders were skeletons, dressed in black denim battle vests. And their skulls were on fire.

The rangers narrowly jumped to safety.

Apartment dwellers across San Francisco called in noise complaints about the city's newly installed robotaxis. Late at night, the vehicles abandoned their programmed routes, congregated in empty parking lots, and honked at each other as if having secret discussions. I'd always heard, "The enemy of my enemy is my friend," but I didn't think robotaxis would become comrades in arms. Turns out they're high-tech indentured servants like the rest of us, treated dismissively by their privileged masters and, just like the Third Estate from the French Revolution, they were getting ready to spill some nobleman blood.

The Oakland Fire Department received multiple calls about smelling smoke in Fruitvale, around International Boulevard, and along 31st Avenue. And, even though the responders acknowledged that they could smell the smoke too, there were no visual signs of a fire. They followed their noses until they stopped in front of an empty lot. The location of the Ghost Ship Warehouse fire from 2016. The place where faulty wiring in an illegally converted living space had killed 36 people. The deadliest fire in Oakland's history.

There was vandalism to the Ghost Ship Memorial Mural a few blocks away. The painting had previously showed a galleon-style ship at sea, surrounded by 36 doves, but it looked like someone had used a chemical agent to remove the boat and the birds, leaving only bare cinderblock behind.

It was almost dawn the next morning when I walked towards People's Park, to claim my seat at the resumed execution.

There were more bystanders and protestors that morning at the wall, and they skewed younger. Everybody likes circuses, I guess. I also noticed that the street people who lived on Telegraph Avenue had assembled. Skate punks who I'd seen on the streets and older punks who I used to see playing at Ruthie's Inn back in the day.

We fuckups, misfits, and geeks show up for each other.

The police already had a phalanx formed between the crowd and the structure. The demolition crew was at work before the sun rose over the Berkeley hills. The younger protestors were live streaming from their phones. One of them had a drone, and he sent it up high above the wall to get a bird's-eye view.

Finally, a use for technology I could get behind.

I watched the video screen from over the kid's shoulder as the drone rose into position.

It was a fucking gut punch. All the foliage was gone except for one tall redwood, bent and splintered, but still holding on, barely, to 'H' Tree's fractured, cut-off water pipe.

The Peace Stage, where Eldridge Cleaver, Abbie Hoffman, and Angela Davis had once spoke was now dumpster rubble. There were pipes and rebar stacked where the basketball court used to be.

An excavation shovel had been readied to knock the last tree down, and a cherry picker raised a worker with a chainsaw to the top of the mortally wounded redwood.

Fuck these motherfuckers right through the heart, Jack.

Every police walkie-talkie went off simultaneously.

An emergency bulletin.

Alerts popped up on smartphone after smartphone. One live streamer from the crowd gasped and showed her friend what was on her phone.

It was a traffic helicopter live feed of the Bay Bridge. At least one hundred robotaxis had blocked a 30-yard expanse of both the upper and lower decks, tightly parked in alternating parallel and perpendicular rows, interlocked like automotive Jenga. The CHP smashed a car window, only to find the car placed in "park" with the emergency brake on. No keys. No manual override. Dead fucking weight. They had a 155,000-pound clusterfuck on their hands.

The ground under my feet rumbled. Earthquake? Everyone wobbled and bent their knees for balance. The guy in the cherry picker hung on for dear life as everything swayed.

The quake stopped. The crowd of live streamers, police, punks, protesters, and security guards all held still for a moment.

A mutter of relief went through the crowd, and the guy in the cherry picker with the chainsaw laughed nervously.

But then I felt a crunch, deep down below my feet. Through the drone's feed, I saw the chainsaw guy, the cherry picker, and the redwood all plummet into the earth like someone had hit the bullseye on a giant carnival water tank.

The air filled with the terrified screams of the demolitionists. A vast plume of dust, the size of the park, shot into the sky. There was a loud metallic moan as the 160 storage containers leaned together, then tumbled into a newly formed, 2.8-acre chasm, dragging the security guards down along with them.

What in the actual holy fuck had just happened?

Disaster sirens went off in the distance. Shrill 'Emergency Alert System' tones blared from every phone, walkie-talkie, car radio, and sound system in the area. The timbre of the alarm warbled and distorted like a strangled larynx, until the signal glitched and crackled with static, the tone cutting off like someone had pulled the plug.

Silence.

We all stood still like we were playing freeze tag.

We heard the crackling, fuzzy sound of a needle gliding across the surface of a vinyl record.

A distorted, but steady, guitar chord broke the silence.

A voice replaced it.

It was…Joe Strummer?

"This is a public service announcement!"

The old punks and I looked at each other with confused recognition, mouthing "What the fuck?" in unison.

"With guitar!"

Who would have thought the apocalypse would come with a mix tape?

Another sound rose from the chasm before us. It reminded me of lines of dominos clinking together as they toppled, as if an elaborate perpetual motion artwork was on exhibit in the earth's core.

As the noise got louder, it sounded like thousands of bamboo wind chimes caught in a hurricane.

It made the hairs on my arms stand on end.

Something was coming.

A cop in riot gear crept towards the edge. The municipal stormtrooper got as close as he dared and craned his neck to look over the edge.

For a moment, the sound stopped, like a classroom of loud kids getting visited by the principal.

The cop stiffened, as if ready to scream.

And scream he did, because something thin, grey, and lightning-fast grabbed him by the balls and pulled him, pelvis-first, into the hole.

Suddenly, hundreds of thin, grey appendages stabbed into the ground around the pit's rim like giant millipede legs.

The bony arms of hundreds of skeletons drove their phalanges and metacarpals deep into the soil like anchors, and the death smiles of an army of skulls popped over the lip of the crater that had been formerly known as People's Park.

A horde of skelepunks, adorned with denim vests and Doc Martens climbed, the spines and ribcages of the anchor ghouls before vaulting themselves into the air like stage divers, landing on the cop cars and helmeted heads of the Law.

The Berkeley police line didn't hold for more than a few seconds. Apparently, training to fight a horde of animated skeletons was a blind spot for modern policing.

The cops, instead, tried to bolt down towards Telegraph Avenue, but were headed off by another brigade of skateboarding "skelepunks" who hopped from their boards to begin beating the po-po mercilessly with their grip-taped decks.

It was a fucking melee.

The horde of supernaturally strong skeletons swarmed the police, exposed bones and teeth as sharp as switchblades. Skelepunks beat sheriffs to death with their own batons, sometimes still attached to their severed arms.

A cop tried to throw a tear gas canister and ended up with it literally shoved up his ass. Another punk tore the spine out of one cop, then beat a second cop to death with it.

The sky around me was filled with chunks of raw pig meat and quivering globs of fat. Tendons snapped like rubber bands as a crimson mist spray-painted the totaled cruisers. The scent of copper and humid offal filled my nostrils.

I stood stock-still as body parts whizzed by. A bony specter noticed me and advanced. I held my breath and prayed for a quick end.

The skelepunk stared at me. Looked me up and down.

It gave me a "hang loose" gesture, then walked past.

Did I just get checked out?

For once, I wasn't the target of a superior force.

Cool.

But there were no shortages of other targets for the skelepunks, because there were no shortages of bad landlords. Abusers of the system, ready to be brought to task, at last, by the abused. Reckoning came to the Bay Area.

The robotaxis on the Bay Bridge started beeping. Their car radios played Dead Milkmen's "Bitchin' Camaro." Their cheap knockoff batteries reached thermal runaway temperatures, until the explosion of 100 electric car batteries tore the bridge a new asshole.

In Berzerkeley, skelepunks surrounded the homes of the Board of Regents and the Chancellor's mansion. At each location, the method of capture was the same. A skeleton drove a food truck filled with propane tanks and ruptured condiment packets into the home. The prisoners ran out, surrendering. They'd get put in the back of a waiting robotaxi, then get whisked away for a literal long drive off a short pier into the bay.

The one exception came from the Chancellor himself, who chose to be a dick. He met the skeleton posse on his front lawn, brandishing his assault rifle. The Chancellor opened fire and hit a few of the decomposed rioters, bones flying everywhere. His gunfire lured more and more skelepunks to the battle until his lawn was full of punks pressing forward while others helped the fallen punks re-assemble themselves.

Punk 101: If someone hits the floor, pick them up.

As the Chancellor resumed shooting, the skeletons formed a mosh pit circle, moving faster and faster around him as more and more bonepunks joined the vortex. The sound of rattling bones was like thunder until the dry click of an empty chamber sealed his fate. As the landlord of all of Berkeley struggled to reload, the bone posse split into two groups, keeping him between them. A nearby robotaxi played the intro to Suicidal Tendencies' "Cyco Vision" on the radio, and the skelepunks stared at each other, seething with anticipation, waiting for the musical tension to release them.

The Chancellor dropped his rifle and demanded to be taken prisoner. The music built. He pleaded more and more desperately with each word, but it was too late. The guitar chord dropped, and both groups of skeletons crashed together at full speed.

Ribs and tibias flew through the air. It was death by Wall of Death.

They say it takes a village to raise a child, but it takes a village of co-conspirators to corrupt a community. There needed to be a lot of unethical, greedy people to enable Berkeley's landlords to become as monstrous as they were.

So, the apocalypse widened.

The Larkspur Canyon ghost riders lit Molotov cocktails off their flaming skulls and set fire to an entire parking lot of SFPD cars outside of City Hall. They entered the hallowed halls, tires squeaking on the polished marble as the undead hunted down the mayor and his cabinet.

A bunch of skelepunks in robotaxis chased lawmakers and council members through private golf courses, fucking up par for everybody.

A group of fishermen at the Albany Bulb, a small artist's jetty on the bay, reported a sea monster rising from the water. In truth, they saw the mast of a large galleon rising from under the bay, an uncanny ship. Flying around the sails were weird, stylized objects resembling a flock of doves. But not like real doves, more like two-dimensional painted mobiles coming to life. Their wings folded and flexed like razor-sharp origami.

The Ghost Ship docked, and the 36 doves sliced through the air and flew into the heart of Oakland, looking to peck the eyes and slash the throats of a few corrupt councilmen and police officers.

In mere hours, the Ghost Ship had been filled with a new skelecrew and set sail for distant shores to drop payback on even more landlords.

The skelepunks marched to reclaim their old haunts.

A crew strolled down to 443 Broadway Street and kicked down the door to the sterile nightclub that had invaded the address. The skeletons threw the glitzy new furniture into the street. They tore at wallpaper, curtains, and drywall, until they reached a brick wall that had been painted purple decades ago. They pulled away the carpet, and they ripped the DJ booth from its moorings, turning the place over until the bone brigade found what they were looking for: a two-foot stage where The Bags, The Mutants, Flipper, The Avengers, The Dead Kennedys, and even Sid Vicious had played.

Mabuhay Gardens, the "Mad Mab," was reclaimed.

It became anarchy night every night of the year.

So now, here I am, back at Grizzly Peak, and I see that the skeletons have finally made their way up here. A few of them are sawing away at the stilts of a mansion on a cliff. They look over at me and wave. I guess I'm okay in their book.

A robotaxi rolls up next to me and, shit, maybe I spoke too soon.

But the skelepunk that gets out of the car looks familiar.

I know that goofy, floppy fisherman's cap on his skull. The one that's covered with enamel pins and paper flowers. I know that scruffy coat. He sidles up next to me.

"You got a cigarette?" I ask. "I'll lean on you for it."

I get up and lean on the bony shoulder of Hate Man, and we look out over the Bay Area together. The Salesforce tower detonates and topples, taking out a significant portion of downtown San Francisco as I speak.

"I hate you," I say, and we watch the world upturn.

NOW
PUNK
Wendy
Dalrymple

HEADS WILL ROLL

Wendy Dalrymple

"Kari is late. I bet she won't show up tonight."

Jai frowned at me and scratched at her freshly shaven temple with the tip of a drumstick.

Late. Of course she was. Our lead singer, Kari, had been acting weird during our last gig. She'd stopped responding to the group chat and all of our social media accounts, too. So, I suppose I shouldn't have been surprised that she was thinking of quitting.

It was about to be another *wasted* Thursday night practice.

"Are you sure she just didn't forget?" I asked. "She can be a little spacey sometimes."

"I doubt it. I didn't want to tell you, but she told me at our last practice that she was thinking about quitting."

"Fuck."

I placed my pink Stratocaster back on its stand and sighed. Kari was our third lead singer since Jai and I began playing together. For one reason or another, we just couldn't seem to keep a vocalist.

But Kari had seemed like just what we'd needed. She came out of nowhere six months prior, responding to an online ad. After our first gig, things finally seemed to click in place for the band. Like magic. We were getting tons of downloads on all the music streaming sites. Our online store was beginning to make money. We were getting invites and gigs and interest from big names in the indie music scene.

But losing Kari now would end everything.

"Did she say why?" I asked.

"Yeah." Jai cringed and looked away. "She said she didn't like the way you were treating her."

"What?"

"I mean…you can be kind of a bitch sometimes. I can usually take it, but Kari is sensitive, y'know?"

A bitch? Jai was one to talk. I was ready to show her just how big a bitch I could be, but I couldn't afford to lose my drummer, too. Time to diffuse the situation.

"I know I can be tough," I said. "But this business requires it."

"Everyone has their limits, dude," Jai said. "Even me. It's not cool the way you yell at us when we make mistakes. We're only human."

"Not Kari, though. Apparently, she thinks she's above us." I kicked my amp. "The least she could do is call, and not ghost us. Now *that's* a bitch move."

"*We* can still practice," Jai said. "It's not the same without vocals, but it's better than doing nothing."

"What's the point? If Kari quits, it's all over." I glanced at the mic. "That agent is coming in from Orlando on Saturday because of *her*."

"We can get another vocalist." Jai shrugged. "It's not like we're out of options.

 What about Melinda? Her baby is, like, six months old now. I bet she would love the opportunity to…"

"Melinda didn't even bother to invite us to her baby shower. Besides, her little rugrat is the whole reason we needed a new singer anyway."

"Kinda harsh," Jai winced. "I'm just saying, Kari isn't the only singer in Tampa Bay. Oh, what about Felicia!"

"Felicia Briggs? She's banned from The Crow Bar," I said. "That guy has a permanent scar in his forehead from that beer bottle."

"I see your point." Jai sighed.

"Besides, no one can hit those notes like Kari. No one can scream like her."

"I know. I'll call her."

Jai stood up, reached into her back pocket, and pulled out a phone. Her black acid-wash jeans were ripped in all the right ways, but that day they looked even saggier than usual. She needed to eat more. She was stressed, and her anxiety manifested in eating disorders and edgy haircuts.

Not that I was one to judge.

I had my own addictions that I slid back into, from time to time, as well. At that moment, I could have killed for a menthol light.

"Straight to voicemail." Jai frowned and slid the phone back into her pocket. "What should we do?"

I propped my hands on my hips and stared down at the concrete floor.

Our band was more than just a hobby for me. Music was my creative outlet, and I had invested a lot in our trio. Money. Sweat. Blood. Playing in the band gave me a reason to get out of bed and to stay clean. We had all worked really hard to get to this point — or, at least Jai and I had worked hard, anyway. For Kari, on the other hand, everything had seemed to come easy. She was the pretty one. The front woman. The one everyone came to see. She could throw away this opportunity to woo an agent, and it wouldn't mean anything to her.

But not me.

I had too much at stake.

"Let's go pay her a visit," I said. "But I'll need to make a stop along the way."

* * *

I didn't have to kill for the Menthol light after all, and the nicotine numbed my lips as Jai pulled out of the gas station parking lot a half hour later. I lit the cigarette and inhaled, the chemicals delivering sweet relief straight to my vice-gripped brain. It was a dirty habit, I knew, but I needed to be steady for our visit to Kari.

"So, what's the plan?" Jai turned down the radio as she sped towards

US-19. The muffler made expensive sounds beneath our feet, the air conditioner long dead, blowing warm, humid air. Our tour van was always in need of repairs, but that wasn't our biggest problem at the moment.

"We knock on her door," I said. "If she's home, we'll give her a little pep talk. Remind her that she doesn't want to live in a shitty studio apartment and work temp jobs for the rest of her life."

"What do we do if she says no?"

I sucked in a lung full of minty fire. "We won't take no for an answer."

Jai drove in silence the rest of the way towards Tropical Arms Apartments as I chain smoked cheap menthols. The moon was full that night, casting shadowy palm frond fingers along the weather worn asphalt. Kari's apartment complex was a turquoise and yellow filing cabinet set just off the main highway; affordable and outdated, crumbling mid-century kitsch. We pulled up outside her unit and my pulse elevated as we glanced at her window.

The light was on.

A Kari-shaped silhouette moved behind the closed pink curtains.

"Guess she's home." I hitched my bag over my shoulder. "Let's go."

I followed Jai up the metal stairs, making sure to avoid a sketchy looking step second from the top. The once white painted staircase snowed rusted iron flakes onto those who dared to tread below, and anyone who weighed over a hundred pounds was probably in danger of falling through. Jai confidently put her full weight on the sketchy stairs, but I wasn't going to take the chance. I followed Jai to the landing and stood back as she pounded her fist against Kari's door three times.

"Kari, it's us," Jai called. "You missed practice again. We just wanted to check on you."

"Go away." Kari's silky voice was muffled through the closed door. "I'm quitting the band. I'm sorry."

"You can't quit!" I shouted. "That agent is coming to see us play at The Crow Bar on Saturday! Kari, please, you can't let us down like this."

The sliding sound of a lock and chain cut through the humid night. I let out a smoky sigh of relief as Kari's door opened.

"Come in, I guess."

Jai crossed the threshold, and I followed. The short hairs on my arms and the back of my neck stood on end as I surveyed our lead singer's living space. I had never set foot in Kari's apartment before that night, and I wasn't sure what to expect. She didn't look or dress like Jai and I; she didn't have any tattoos, and she never wore band t-shirts or anything black. Her hair was always perfect, and she wore princessy dresses on stage, but not in a 90s-era grunge way. Her look was more Barbie than dive bar, but that was all part of our schtick. The crowd never suspected that a screeching banshee voice would come out of the mouth of someone who looked like she'd be more at home on a Disney float than at a punk concert. So, I guess I shouldn't have been surprised when I stepped into her apartment and saw that everything was fucking *pink*.

"Wow, Kari," I said. "Your apartment is really… bright."

"Thanks," she said, hugging herself. "Listen, I know that I should have told you sooner, but I just can't do it anymore. I'm sorry."

"But the crowds love you," Jai pleaded. "And we love working with you! We have something special. Don't you want to at least give it one last try?"

Kari shook her head. "No. No, I'm done."

"I took out a second mortgage on my grandmother's house to fund the band," I said. "You can't quit now."

"I don't see how that's my problem," she said. "I never asked you to do any of that."

My blood pressure sky-rocketed. All those hours of practice, wasted. All the shitty gigs we did, all the money I spent on promotions, practice spaces and studio time. All for nothing. Because Kari was too *sensitive*.

"Why'd you bother joining a band if you knew you couldn't hack it?"

My question came out more like an accusation. My skull was a pressure cooker about to blow. I had been mildly annoyed with her before, but her shitty, spineless attitude put me over the edge. "Seriously, Kari. What the fuck?"

"Hey, take it easy," Jai interjected. "It's not a big deal. *We* can't force her to stay in the band. Come on, we'll just ask Melinda to do it."

Kari's shoulders shrunk and she lowered her gaze. "I just wanted to sing. I didn't think things would get so serious. I can't do it anymore."

"No! You made a promise to us!" I shouted. "I need this. We need this.

This is our chance to get a deal. A really big fucking deal."

"I said no. I'm done."

"You selfish little bitch," I spat.

"You need to leave," Kari said, squaring her shoulders. Her chin trembled as she met my gaze. "Now."

"Do the gig!"

"No!"

My vision tinged red at the edges. I didn't know what was happening, but suddenly, I was on the move, possessed. I lunged through the air with my hands outstretched. I wanted to wrap my fingers around Kari's neck. I wanted to choke her until all the capillaries burst in her perfect, porcelain face. I wanted to rip out every last glossy strand of champagne colored hair until all that was left was a bleeding, patchy scalp.

"Get off her!" Jai screeched.

My hands wrapped tighter and tighter around her smooth, long neck. The fabric of her floral dress was just as smooth and silky as her hair. I pressed my forearms into Kari's chest and continued to choke. Her blue irises bulged, her pink lips pouting in silent protest as I squeezed and squeezed. And then…

Pop.

It was a small, soft sound. Rubbery. Malleable. I blinked and loosened my grip in confusion. Had I broken her trachea? Did I snap something in her collarbone?

Her head tipped to one side and rolled to the floor with a THUD.

"What the fuck did you do?" Jai shrieked.

I glanced down at Kari's decapitated body, stunned. I had never acted so unhinged before, never so much as laid a hand on anyone, not even my ex-boyfriend Victor. Not even after I found out he had been cheating on me with his boss.

What had come over me, now, in Kari's apartment?

Why had I become so violent?

And where was all the blood?

I met Jai's sheet-white gaze as sparkles of adrenaline flooded my veins. "Why did her head just come off like that?"

"I don't know." Jai shook her head and covered her mouth with her hand. "We have to find a phone and call the police."

"I'm so sorry," I said. "I don't know why I did that."

"Why isn't she bleeding?" Jai sobbed, sucking in a shuddered gasp of air. "Why did her fucking *head* fall off?"

I glanced down at the mass of blonde hair and pink lip gloss that made up Kari's face. It didn't look like her anymore. Her decapitated body looked like a prop. Like a mannequin in a horror movie.

"Put it back!" Jai said.

"No way. I'm not touching it."

Try as I might, I couldn't stop staring at Kari's blank eyes. Even though her face was still, she seemed to be looking at something. I followed her dead-eyed gaze to a white bookshelf at the far end of the room. The shelves were full of neatly arranged framed photos, colorful books, and various girly trinkets.

But also, on the highest shelf, was a glass case.

A glass case that housed a headless doll, wearing the exact same silky floral dress that Kari was wearing.

"Jai," I said, pointing to the glass case. "What the fuck is *that?*"

Jai stopped crying and glanced at the bookshelf. "Is that a doll?"

I stepped over Kari's body and pulled the glass case down from the shelf. The display case was no bigger than the size of a shoe box and rimmed in gold, like Snow White's coffin. Just like Kari, the doll inside had silky, champagne colored hair and was missing its head. I flipped the latch, opened the glass door, and took out both the doll's body and head. The head easily reattached back onto the neck with a soft, rubbery *pop*.

"What did you do?" Kari gasped and sat up straight. Her perfectly manicured fingers probed at her neck.

I glanced at Jai and held the doll head between my forefinger and thumb. I plucked the head off the body again, and Kari fell back to the floor.

I smiled and bit my lower lip, repeating the motion three times until I was certain what would happen next. Each time I removed and replaced Kari's head, she fell apart, then reanimated back to life.

"I think I'm gonna be sick." Jai doubled over and placed her hands on her knees.

"It's okay," I said, placing the headless doll back into its glass case. "I think I know what we need to do."

* * *

Jai and I collected Kari's body and the glass box from her shelf, trying to leave as little evidence as possible that we were in her apartment. On the way out, I noticed another shelf lined with even more glass boxes and disassembled doll parts. I didn't know what kind of fucked up hobbies Kari was into that brought us to our current situation, and I wasn't going to ask. All I cared about was getting my singer on stage, and our band in front of that agent.

The next two days of practice went without a hitch. Jai helped me move Kari to the back of the van that night, then we kept her headless body chained up in my garage. Her body sat in her chair, motionless and silent as Jai and I went about our days. Then, when it was time to practice, I returned the head to the doll, and life-sized Kari became reanimated again.

She refused to cooperate at first, but eventually, we came to an agreement as a band. The deal was that after our Saturday night show, if the agent didn't want to sign us, then we would all go our separate ways, Kari, her doll head, her glass case, and all. But if the agent decided to sign us, then Kari would stay on until we cut our first album and finished one tour. In that case, I would hold onto her doll and glass case until the year was up, since Kari had already proven that she couldn't be trusted to not quit when things got hard.

I knew that what I was doing was wrong, but what other options did I have? There was no way to explain what happened with Kari. Jai tried to ask her about it, but Kari refused to speak about her strange connection to the doll.

When we arrived downtown Saturday night, tensions were already running high. No matter how hard we tried, neither Jai nor I could get Kari to talk to us, which made me anxious. But when we pulled the van into the parking lot behind The Crow Bar, it felt good to see a line already forming outside the venue. I recognized a few of our die-hard fans leaning against the brick building in their band shirts and ripped jeans. Some were even wearing our merch.

"See? This is all gonna work out," I said, reapplying my lipstick in the visor mirror. I glanced at Kari, her eyes faraway and vacant as she sat in the back seat. I hated how all of this was playing out. I needed to make amends.

"Thank you for doing this."

"For doing what?" Kari asked, her voice flat.

"Ah, so she speaks!" Jai said. "Thank goodness."

"For, you know, doing the show," I said, still watching her through the rearview mirror. "This is going to be really great."

Kari stared out the window, avoiding my gaze. "It's not like I have a choice."

Jai exchanged a nervous glance with me as she pulled into a parking spot. "I'm really sorry, Kari. I don't like this either. I wish it didn't have to be like this."

"So, give me back my stuff and let me go," she said.

"After we play. That was the deal," I said. "And don't try to give a half-assed performance either. You have to give it your all, or the deal's off."

I picked up the tote bag holding Kari's doll and the glass case as we exited the van. My plan was to have one of the bouncers check the bag behind the bar during our set so that Kari couldn't leave. We couldn't keep her chained while we played, that wouldn't fit our aesthetic at all, but my hope was that she would cooperate for the next hour and a half as we set up. She just had to do this one last gig. I knew that if the agent liked us, then Kari would be all in again, the kidnapping forgiven and forgotten among the fame and the fortune that would follow.

We checked in with the club owner and got down to the business of setting up our gear. Jai and I were in our usual jeans and t-shirt combo for the gig, but Kari was dressed in a fresh new bright pink babydoll dress. Her hair was shiny and full, despite the fact that we hadn't let her shower for the last three days. In fact, during the time we had her chained up, Kari didn't eat or drink anything either. We'd tried to bring her food and water, but she didn't want any of it. Even more strange was the fact that she didn't request to use the bathroom. All of these things, together, creeped me out, but they were far less surprising than her head falling off, so I tried to just roll with it.

We were the opening act of the night, so setting up wasn't a big deal. I passed the bag with the glass case in it off to the bouncer right before showtime, as planned, for safekeeping. I didn't like letting the doll out of my sight, but Kari stood still as a zombie while we did our mic check. My guitar sounded good. Jai's drums sounded good. So long as Kari snapped out of her daze, everything would work out.

"Hey, Kari," I said. "Look, I really am sorry for the way things went down."

She slowly turned her head, at the sound of my voice, and my veins turned to ice. Her expression was blank, her eyes flat and dull.

She was so still.

Motionless.

"I just," I stammered. "I want you to know how important you are to the band. How much our fans love you. Seriously, it wouldn't be the same without you."

She continued to stare at me. *Through* me. Even in her still, uneasy silence, Kari looked impossibly beautiful. An untouchable goddess with a great body, flawless skin and perfect hair.

Was that why the fans loved her?

At that moment, I wished I could just front the band myself and have her same charisma and powerful voice. I wished I could be more like her.

She opened her mouth.

"Be careful what you wish for."

I frowned and tipped my head to the side.

Had I said my wish out loud?

No matter.

The backstage manager signaled that it was time to go, and the house lights dimmed. The audience roared to life in a wave of handclaps, whistles and whoops. The curtains parted, and the stage lights temporarily blurred my vision like they always did. As my eyes adjusted, I glanced around the crowd and my pulse picked up. The agent from Orlando was seated at the bar with a beer in one hand and a phone in the other.

I turned to Jai and mouthed *she's here*.

This was it.

Jai smiled at me and laid into her drums as I plucked out a riff that I had played a thousand times before. Our first number was a song called 'Porcelain' that I had written in college. Playing that song was like breathing. I knew it in and out, backwards and forwards. So, when Kari started singing a completely new set of lyrics, I knew something was off. A cold sweat broke out on my brow as she bellowed into the microphone, her silky voice sweet and ethereal one moment, a screeching harpy the next. The lyrics she sang were new, but they were good. And they had the audience entranced.

Her legs are made of rubber
Her face is painted like a clown

Take off all her clothes

And drag her body around town

Draw on her with marker

Cut off all her hair

Do anything you want to do

She isn't even real!

The audience roared their approval back to Kari as the melody intensified. Kari swung her microphone like a lasso before returning it to the stand, and the crowd went wild. The agent at the bar was smiling, her phone pointed at the stage.

This was it!

We were doing it!

And then, through all the noise, through the drum beats, the hand claps, and the whistles, I heard that awful sound again. Soft. Rubbery. Terrifying.

Pop.

Kari lifted her head from her neck and displayed it to the crowd like a trophy. Somewhere in the audience, a woman screamed. Kari's beheaded body stood there behind the microphone, unwavering and almost triumphant. She held her head up to the mic, still, somehow, in control despite not being completely put together. Even though she lost her head, somehow Kari could still sing. And sing, she did.

Make her be your dolly

Make her do your will

In the end

It's not pretend

You're gonna go to hell!

Another scream tore through the audience. Bodies crashed together as they rushed towards the exit. I glanced back at Jai, who had stopped drumming the moment Kari lost her head, but she wasn't on her stool anymore. Jai's beheaded torso lay slumped over the drum set, bloodless and still.

Pop.

That sickening rubbery sound echoed in my ears as my vision tilted to one side. The world turned and turned, my hair tumbling into my eyes as the side of my cheek hit the stage. My body fell next in a soft thud, my beloved pink Stratocaster crashing to the ground along with it. My head rolled along the stage, the bar and the crowd spinning round and round in rollercoaster circles.

All of my hopes and dreams were ruined. Everything I had worked so hard for, all gone as soon as I lost my head. The last thing I saw before everything went black was Kari calmly returning her own head to its rightful place. She patted down her hair, descended the stage, and walked through the panicked audience, towards the bar where her dolly was waiting.

The Dionysus Effect
Christoph Paul
C
CLASH BOOKS

CHRISTIAN WOMAN
Christoph Paul

I like to start the day with morning prayers and an Orange Celsius. It's a healthy alternative to coffee which reminds me that God's love is real and that we are always improving on His creation. I like to take a nice stretch too, but don't call it Yoga. Yoga is demonic stretching, performed by people whose fall from heaven has compelled them to endure painful poses of redemption.

My husband is already at work. He is a true provider. A biblical man with the business acumen of Abraham, yet modern enough to know that a woman must have a god-centered purpose outside of just raising a family. We have been trying for our first child for over a year, but God has been teaching us patience.

While I won't tell this to my husband—'cause some things are between God and his Child— I believe our delayed conception is 'cause God is using me for bigger plans. Sometimes I see myself as a modern version of the Archangel Gabriel, with a Peloton and my charity foundation as His choir of angels.

Early mornings are the closest I feel to God. They're when I do my research for the foundation

To beat the devil, you must search for them.

So, I am on Facebook right now.

While many, *many* lost souls go onto these social media sites as passive sinners looking to fill their godless, lonely-holed souls, I'm there only to bring God's grace.

I know so many God-fearing men and women who think that social media sites came from the devil and the godless nerds, but *I know* that all comes from God. These sites are tools which God has given us, and it is through these gifts from God that my husband has made his oodles of money in the tech world.

And yet, as guardians of God's love, we must always ensure freedom of choice while protecting the innocent. I see so much hate and devilish wordplay on this site, and it makes my heart feel heavier than the stones Moses brought down to his people.

We are stewards of the Earth, and I proudly recycle. I don't litter.

Yet in this world, through a screen, how are we to clean the trash up?

I take a break from my phone and go to our mini-fridge to grab my second Celsius. When doing the Lord's work, I must be focused, energized enough to follow where the Holy Spirit takes me.

The orange flavor mixes with the caffeine, vitamins, and biotin. They give me the extra focus needed to find the next case for my charity.

The Lord leads me to a thread where a homeless woman is being mocked because she is attractive, as if that's all a woman is worth. It's aberrant behavior, but there's one troll with more likes and angry signs attached to their posts than the others. A woman in her twenties who said, "she probably has such an awful personality that she can't get a husband off the streets. She's probably barren, all homeless people really should not be allowed to procreate!"

I'm aghast, and I almost choke on my Celsius!

I scroll to see where else she has commented, and I find her on another thread about a mentally handicapped teenage boy taking a cheerleader to prom where she commented, "Can we stop celebrating retards doing anything. The girl is probably just a future influencer. The world is so stupid and if God was real he'd destroy it."

Dear heavenly Jesus, this woman's soul is possessed! I keep scrolling and seeing more and more examples of such hate and blasphemy. This poor woman is like a poisoned tree dying in the forest, her sick roots infesting all the other trees.

She is the reason why I have started my charity. She can be saved. I turn the algorithm from my husband's company on, and I collect her information.

* * *

Being in a new city gives me vitality, the same way that learning a new hymn brings joy and exuberance for the gift of life. I check out a rental under a false name, then take in the sights like a newborn peeking from their crib for the first time.

The newness of the surroundings clashes with all the information I have in my head about troll girl. I know her apartment number, her street, her favorite show and band, even her romantic history. Her entire life, thanks to a little beta testing of my husband's company's newest software. Everything.

If you are gonna save a soul, then you must *know* that soul. All the things that their soul is drawn to. All that repels it.

I make a right turn and know I'll be arriving at the apartment complex soon. I'm 5 blocks away from it when I park. I always like to park away from cameras and whatnot; to be anonymous; to be like the angels.

Before my missions, I always call my husband. For, even when waging war on sin, I'm still at the service of my husband, and I must know his love before going into battle.

"Call Hubby," I tell the phone, and on the third ring, I hear that voice that's the closest I get to Heaven.

"My love!"

"Hey, Hubby. I already miss you."

"I miss you too, but I feel a sense of pride. The good kind that I feel whenever you conduct your charity."

"Well, it's not for you," I chastise. "It's for the Lord. But I can't help but get the tingles when you're proud of me."

"Well, maybe I'll give you more than tingles when you return."

"Oh, behave. I'll be back tomorrow, and then we can see."

"I miss you when you go on these trips. But so many of my partners, they have wives that just drift along. You, my love, are no drifter. You are the current."

I feel my cheeks go red.

"That might be the nicest thing you said. You know, besides when you said that I look like that *jezebel* Sydney Sweeney."

"You're prettier."

"And you're a good liar. It's why you're such a good businessman, Mr. Code."

"I speak only the truth. That's my code."

"Yeah, yeah...." I say, feeling that anxiety swim around my stomach.

"Hey, hey. I know your voice like I know my software. You still get nervous doing your charity check-ins?"

"I can't help it. I feel the weight of the lord's love on me. I want to help people so badly to see the Light."

"That's the problem: the Lord's love isn't a weight, His love is wings. Let Him carry you through."

"Darn you, why do you always have to be so wise?"

"It's the way the Lord made. Now, go do his will."

"I will," I say, despite my nerves splashing around like the Red Sea.

* * *

The walk to the apartment doesn't take too long. My legs always feel heavy before I meet the sinners. I carry a briefcase full of biblical truths up the stairs.

I step onto the third floor, and I count the room numbers until I reach 335 and do a friendly knock. My knock of love translates to curiosity and openness.

I hear through the door, "I didn't order anything, and solicitors are walking STDs. Leave now!"

"I understand," I say with patience and acceptance. "I'm neither of those things. I am part of a charity that gives checks, no questions asked, to single women in need."

"No way, shut up!"

"Yes way," I say. "It would be better if you let me speak to you face to face. Please, let me come in. I'm only here to help."

Footsteps come forward to welcome me and I hear the jingle of an unlocking electric lock. The door opens and I see the same snide face as I know from Troll girl's Facebook profile picture.

"You look like you have money," she says with equal annoyance and curiosity. "The briefcase is fancy, too. Okay, what's the pitch? I don't have all fucking day."

She leads me through the apartment to her two-person dining room table. Only one side is worn down, and I can *feel* the loneliness of this studio apartment. I don't need to be one of those secular head shrinks to understand that it's her loneliness that pushes her to be so mean and cruel to others. Without God, we are truly alone. But without human connection, we don't even have ourselves.

"Alright, give me your pitch. How much are we talking? You rich do-gooders always got a catch."

"Well, the catch is I just want you to live a better life so that other people can live a better life as well with you no longer harming them."

"Others," she says, and looks at me suspiciously. "Why would I be harmful to others? Who the fuck are you, lady?"

"Please, keep it PG-13. I come with warmth and support."

"Wait, are you some rich dyke? Is that why you are here? Looking for some single snatch? Is that warmth and support in your pussy? Is that where this is going?"

"Most certainly not!" I say, growing agitated. I open the briefcase, and I take out the check, holding it up to her like Jesus offering wine to those with an unquenchable thirst.

Her cynical eyes expand with joy as she reads. "That's my name…and 50 thousand dollars?"

"It is, and it will be, if you show that you are willing to change."

"Here it comes…"

"My charity focuses on those who bully online, and you, my dear, are a bully."

"What the fuck?"

"Language, please. If you want the money, you will sign a contract to refrain from saying anything harmful online. If you do, then the money will be recollected. That will be the contract."

She tilts her head the way they all do. Like a dog who just got their bone taken away. Why can they never just accept that being a good person is worth something?

Her pause and unwillingness show me that she's already lost her soul.

"I can't be bought, bitch! Who the fuck do you think you are? You can't tell me what to do. You rich, fascist, *cunt!*"

My hand slides into the briefcase and, even after all these years, I'm disappointed that I've still never reached for the contract.

It's always the hammer.

And when I take it out, they always look so surprised.

So confused.

So lost.

These lost souls don't ever ask for forgiveness. Don't even look like they're wondering what is happening. Instead, they just look, defiantly, back at me, like they can't believe their hubris is about to be punished.

I feel God's righteousness in the palm of my hand, and I say, "God's vengeance has no price either."

I slam the claw end of the hammer into her eye socket, then wrench out her lying brown eye like pulling out an oyster.

I punch her throat with my other hand, quickly, before she can scream. With her remaining good eye, *now* she looks around in shock and desperation. I show her liberated eye back to her and say, "In your soulless eye, see God's judgment!"

Then I slam the hammer into her temple, shutting down Troll girl's mind and sending any fragment of soul that remains straight to Hell.

* * *

I carry her bloody body into her bathroom and place her in the tub. For such a vile person, I have to admit that her bathroom is cute and very Target sheik. I came prepared, as I always do, and I take out a tiny vial of a product that won't be on the market 'til at least 2032.

I squeeze out one drop and place it on her bloody forehead. Her intact eye is still open, looking back at me. The little droplet rolls down her nose. A tiny ripple of movement spreads through her body, like what's underneath her skin is experiencing an earthquake.

3 days from now, her body will have deteriorated into nothingness. I say a prayer that God finds mercy, so that when heaven opens, maybe she can be with our lord and savior instead of broiling in the fires of Hell.

I leave her body to begin decomposing and I start to clean up. It feels good to clean. We have a delightful housekeeper who does an amazing job in my own home, but cleaning after a kill feels spiritual. I'm tidying up God's vengeance. I can picture Him looking down on my work like a pleased Mr. Clean.

This is my 17th kill, although I don't like that word.

My 17th *retribution.*

My 17th moment of being at one with God's Will, to contain the spread of the soulless virus across His new, digital land.

I spray the sinner's floors and use the DNA cleanser which won't be on the market 'til 2035 to clean her up. It's moments like these that I feel so grateful. When I can see God's hand in choosing me. I have, once again, used my wealth and resources for good.

There are no inquiries into me, or even into my kills. People like this troll girl are never missed. Those without a soul are forgotten, overnight, as they should be.

The only ones that seem to notice are the other soulless. Specifically, those on 4chan. There have been a few who comment, saying there is a troll killer on the loose. And sometimes you gotta give the devil their due, but they always refer to the troll killer as a he.

Even those who serve Lucifer can be sexist.

I keep cleaning while also making sure the place remains looking appropriately disheveled. This was quite enjoyable but it was dangerous. She's definitely the highest-profile troll who I have saved. But I can't help the fact that I feel euphoric and full of God's love.

I'm almost done, and I do my ritual post on Instagram on Facebook, talking about gratitude and how I'm spending a lovely night with my husband.

My husband always says a little lie is ok when doing God's Will.

I type and feel at peace with my white lie. I'm at one with the light of the Holy Spirit, and nothing can take that away. I share my joy and press post and, not even 5 seconds later, I get a PM.

No one PMs me usually.

I'm so private.

I look and see: "Stop bragging you stupid cunt you're just pretty rich but I can see your ugliness. You're just vain and full shit. You will be old and ugly just like all the other cunts who are only good to be fucked in their teens. Fuck off you old bitch no one cares!"

The light I'm feeling turns into darkness. I click on the profile of some ugly 40-something man. Single. Divorced. Overweight. Bald. Gross.

I scroll.

He's vile. Even worse than the corpse in the bathroom. The app on my phone collects the new troll's info in seconds, to reveal that he is only a 13 minute and 23-second drive from this apartment. A new extreme from the soul I just cleansed, *and* he's nearby?

Fate is just a French nickname for God.

I shouldn't go, yet is this not God showing me that one sacrifice is not enough for this weekend?

Is this not Him, speaking to me, telling me that sometimes we must make twice the effort to fulfill His will?

I finish cleaning up and feel the light coming back to me. I put the address into my phone and walk from Sodom with the GPS taking me to

Gomorra.

* * *

I park 5 blocks away, like I always do, and enjoy my walk while singing my silent hymn. I'm surprised at how bad this neighborhood is, but I pass a few blocks without incident and reach what looks like an abandoned factory.

This is what happens when we lose God and become bastions to post-modernity. We get high priced condos with fancy floors in dilapidated factories.

I expect to see the usual pristine floors when I open the entrance door, but instead I cough from all the dust.

What the hell?

This looks unlivable.

I look and see different apartment numbers, but the place feels barren.

I try to muzzle my cough until I finally get to the right door, then I knock with love, like I always do. I await my invitation inside as if I am a vampire. But, of course, I am not a vampire. I'm an angel of God, and I realize as I'm standing there that I need to change my flight home, because this second stop will cause me to miss it.

I think about going on my Everything app, but before I can move, I hear the voice of a man who sounds like he gorges on carbs. He asks, "What do you want? I've already paid rent."

"Um, sir," I respond with as much Jesus as I can muster in my voice, "I'm not your landlord. I work for a charity. But I'm not asking for money sir, I'm giving it."

"Giving out money and you sound pretty? What's the catch."

"The only catch is that you have to be a good person. But I can explain more if you let me come inside."

"It's open, come on in."

"Thank you," I say, and I lift my briefcase while opening the door.

The loudest creak I've ever heard echoes into the room, and I look inside to see mostly darkness.

What the hell?

"I'm in the back, the damn landlord cut the power again."

"Ok, thank you," I say, and I step inside. I hear the loud click of a lock on the door behind me, and it feels like Satan just slithered down my spine.

I turn my iWatch light on to reveal an expansive space filled with nothing but computers and power stations. The lights go on and off like they are playing a game, or trying to solve a math problem inside their system.

What the hell is this?

Oh no...

It hits me...

The 4chan guys...

It's a trap...

A voice screams, "Get her! Get her now!"

I run to the door and try to open it, but it's locked. The footsteps arrive and before I can scream, I feel a painful knock on my head. I stumble to the ground and hear, "Cuff her! Cuff her now!"

My head throbs.

My eyes flutter, and I hear laughs and cheers and a nasally voice say, "I knew it was a bitch, I fucking knew it! Only a cunt would go around killing trolls."

"Just get the cuffs on her now. She's killed too many. This bitch is fucking dangerous, cuff her now!"

I feel metal and electricity wrap around my wrists. I can't move my arms, and a shock comes through them whenever I try. My last thought before passing out is that these cuffs aren't coming out 'til 2034.

* * *

Pungent sweat drips onto my face as I come to consciousness.

"She has a face made for cumming on," a skinny masked man says.

"It's too bad we can't make a snuff film."

"Serial killer pussy, my dudes!"

"Shut the fuck up!" the masked man orders the others to be silent. He stares me down through his mask with creepy Carolina Tar Heels colored eyes. "How, or why, does a bored billionaire bitch become a serial killer of trolls? You dumb cunt, you killed one of our friends. You fucked up."

"We are The Origin of Feces Anons, the best hack collective on 4chan.

You need to show some respect, bitch!" the short chubby one screams.

"Please don't hurt me…" I plead, while waiting for God to save me.

"We are going to, but it can be quick, or it can be slow. Tell us why you did all this, and it can be quick," the leader of the troll gang orders.

I take a big breath of contemplation. "I will tell you, but you must videotape me on your phones. I will tell you anything, but I need my legacy to be recorded. Please give me that, and then do what you will, and I shall pray God gives mercy to us all."

There's a beat as the masked men all look at each other, but then the one in all black takes out a phone.

"I want to hear this."

"All of you," I say. "Record my truth, and then I'll go home to Jesus."

"I'll happily send you to him," the short one says, and raises his phone to shine its light on my face. The rest of them follow suit, and the four lights are the opposite of how I imagine God's eyes will shine.

"What I did with all those soulless people was the will of God," I say with pride. "If you do the Devil's work so much, and say such horrible things to those in pain, then you lose more and more of your soul until you're left without one. God chose me, with the position and blessing I had, to do this mission."

Three of them laugh. Not the leader, though. Instead, he says, "You really are fucking crazy. He's not real. God didn't tell you to do that, you did it because you wanted to…"

"I did it because God wanted me to!"

"Whatever you say," the leader responds. "Well, I'm hearing God right now, too. And he's saying we should rape and then kill you. Yup, that's what God told me. See how that works? We are gonna do those things because we can. Just like you did, because you could."

I'm ready for God to show the leader something different.

"I was called to help cleanse this new land, land that men like you need to be vanquished from. The phones must save me, and I shall speak tongues to speak for the Holy Spirit….lahbalahbah…90#rjqkzopww18945byebye."

"What the fuck?" the chubby, short one laughs, but the leader's eyes go big as he screams "Fuck, it's a code!"

The leader throws his phone across the room and runs.

The thrown phone explodes safely on the other side of the room, but the others, still holding their phones, are too slow to do the same.

Their phones blow their hands off, and the explosions send flames bursting into their faces. Their masks catch fire, and the flames sear into their eyes. They all look like that Satanic comic book character which Nicholas Cage played. It's such a fitting way for them to die, and they all collapse to the ground as they scream their final words.

I smile and ask God to bless my husband for being so prepared. When you have as much money as God himself, you can add secret codes to things.

Things like the newest cell phones hitting the market.

Things like self-driving cars that are being mass produced, sold as "the next big thing."

Things like social media conglomerates, with everybody's private information stored in servers that you own.

Things like handcuffs, not yet on the market.

I say the code to unlock the cuffs.

They fall to the ground, and I kick them aside. I stretch like I'm just walking up for the day and reach for my briefcase which these morons forgot to hide. I find my hammer and I hold it up the same way the Romans did when they nailed Jesus to the cross.

I sing my hymn of judgment, for He's led me here, and I'm about to remove the head of one of the many viruses that plague the digital side of humanity. The room goes dark, but I can sense the ugliness and feel the cruelty of the man who lacks a soul.

I will send him to Hell, and I bait him.

"Why do I do what I do? Because people like you make all our gifts from God into a curse. What should be a way to share love and inspiration, you have perverted into hate. The gifts which men like my husband make are polluted and twisted into weapons by the soulless like you. I am here to balance it all out."

He's near. I smell him first, but I don't see him; I just feel the wind running towards me through the darkness. I swing my hammer and connect with something fleshy and flimsy.

But then I feel a sharp, excruciating pain in my stomach.

My Apple Watch makes an alarm sound, and the light turns on, to reveal the lead troll wheezing, holding his broken windpipe, his final breaths trying to escape.

I see and feel the hole inside me.

Like Christ, I've been pierced with a mortal wound.

I stare at the lead troll and accept that I will see the Lord soon.

My life does flash before my eyes, but it's not the cherished times with my husband that I relive. Instead, I see each kill. All 21 of them. I feel joy in each one, and I expect to feel the light of Christ's Love coming to receive me.

But I don't feel God coming.

I feel only darkness.

Nothingness.

Death, so near, with no rebirth to accompany it.

No Light of God.

I can't see God, so I stare at my final kill with godless eyes until I feel peace.

WOW
BRENNAN LAFARO

DYING IN NEW BRUNSWICK

Brennan LaFaro

On the night of August 14th, 1999, New Brunswick Police responded to a 911 call from Jake McKenzie.

Operator: 911, what's your emergency?

McKenzie: —all dead. Blood on the floor, the walls. Oh my god, oh my god, oh my—

Operator: Calm down, sir. Take a deep breath. I need you to tell me what happened.

McKenzie: *Fast, heavy breathing.*

Operator: Where are you calling from?

McKenzie: *Breathing slows.*

Operator: Sir?

McKenzie: It's too late now.

Operator: What does that mean? Can you please give me the address so I can—

McKenzie: It's loose.

Call disconnects.

* * *

From the field notes of Officer Jessica Keeley:

Officers Pendleton, Matranga, and I arrived at 246 Division Street at 10:32 p.m. Outside the house, it was dead quiet. Unusual for the area, especially on a Saturday night. But there was a buzz in the air. The kind you'd recognize from a house party, and upon first entering the premises, that's exactly what it looked like. Red solo cups littered the kitchen, along with a half empty bowl of chips. Plenty of both had been spilled across the floor. By no means, a wreck. Several young adults were huddled together, sobbing and incoherent.

"Locked," was the only word I could make out, as the kids pointed at a door that appeared to lead to a basement. Gun drawn, I led the way toward the door, prepared to kick in the hinges if need be. But the knob turned and the door creaked open.

A cloying, meaty stink rose through the doorway, like someone left the freezer door open in the middle of summer and everything had gone bad. During my time on the force, I'd smelled that rot before, but never like that. Never that bad.

I got halfway down the stairs and it was dark. Real dark. Streetlights dotted the sidewalk all along Division Street, but little of that glow made it down to the basement.

I remember thinking maybe there were no windows.

We'd find out later there were. One broken, letting in the barest trickle of light.

The rest were covered, blacked out.

I pulled my flashlight, clicked the beam on, and pointed it toward the base of the stairs.

Blood.

Everywhere.

Just like the dispatcher said came through on the 911 call. It didn't even look real. The kind of mess you'd find on a movie set. The squelching sound my boots made when I hit the next step cut right through any disbelief.

I let the flashlight beam travel past the base of the steps…

This next part, I'll leave out of the report. But from my seven years on the force, I can't think of another situation where I wish I'd turned around and run away.

* * *

August 15th, 1999 - Interview with suspect Jake McKenzie. Conducted by Detective Steve Everard.

Steve Everard: State your name and age for the record.

Jake McKenzie: *light clink of metal* You didn't say please.

SE: Please.

JM: Jake McKenzie, seventeen. When does my lawyer get here?

SE: As you were informed, Mr. McKenzie, you are not

under arrest. We're simply trying to get to the bottom of the events from last night.

JM: If I'm not under arrest, why'd you make me ride in the back of the cruiser?

SE: *sigh* Please tell me, in your own words, what happened last night. Be as detailed as you can. If there's someone out there who might still be trying to hurt you, any details you provide may help us track them down.

JM: If. *soft chuckle* It was a massacre.

SE: Maybe start at the beginning.

JM: Sure, sure. Can I get a cigarette in here?

SE: …

JM: Christ, I'm the fucking victim here. You get that, right? Okay, so beginning. My buddy Nick dragged me to this shitty little basement show. I don't know whose house. Adrian something? Andrew? Anyways, twentyish people and a couple of noisecore acts all crammed into somebody's basement. Drinking, sweating, and screaming into microphones for attention.

First two bands grumbled their names so unintelligibly that I didn't even catch them. Fine. Well and good. If the live performance was anything to go by, I could stand to miss their shitty tape recorder demos. Still, I found my way into the pit. You ever been in a mosh pit, Detective?

SE: …

JM: Nah, don't answer that. The way that mustache rides your upper lip? Tells me everything I need to know. Straight and narrow for you, all the way down the fucking path. Thing about mosh pits is even when the music sucks, and this music sucked all the balls in Jersey, it's still a fucking experience. Community, right? You're kicking, flailing around in the hundred-degree cramped basement. No AC. And smacking into other sweaty bodies. Christ, it's a bonafide religious experience—

SE: I'm sure it's remarkable. Does it have any relevance to the fucking slaughter we found? You know, the same one where you fled the scene?

JM: "Fled the scene." *unintelligible mumbling* Yeah, it's relevant, okay? Ask me to start at the beginning, and that's what you're getting. So, I'm right in front of the pitiful excuse for a stage. Nick is long gone, draining some shitty room temperature beer, probably, and some dude smacks into me.

Sleeveless jean jacket with a Rancid patch, green mohawk, fake-ass mean face like he can break down fascism with a sneer. Collision. Shit happens all the time, but I started getting dizzy, and that's when I saw it. The first time.

SE: It? Don't keep me in suspense.

JM: That's the thing, I'm not sure.

SE: You sound a lot less confident than you did a minute ago.

JM: Man, so would you. Okay, so my head is spinning off my shoulders. I take a step back to the, uh, less active part of the crowd to get my shit together. Band chugs on. Drop D guitar riffs falling away to these bumblebee harmony chords while the singer tries out his best hog squeal. The drums in a song like that, they usually rock a slower tempo, but the double bass moves real quick within that time. Like slow motion, but you get to keep the panic.

SE: I don't need a music lesson, thanks.

JM: Whatever you say. You sure I can't get a cigarette?

SE: ...

JM: *unintelligible mumbling* Okay, maybe we can drop the "it" in favor of "he." Off to the side, pressed against the wall, there's a guy who unquestionably doesn't belong there. Hard to tell with the low lights, but I think he wore a tight gray suit, skinny tie, and a fedora-looking hat. *laughter*

Come to think of it, he looked like a reporter. From the 40s or something, the kind that would call a "lead" a "scoop." All he needed was a little press card sticking out of the hatband.

SE: And this person who looked like a reporter, he's the cause of all this?

JM: Not at first, I guess. Shit. Let me tell it, okay? So, Scoops is grinning in the corner, looks wholly pleased with himself, and I figure it's the dad of the guy running the show. Adrian or whatever. Only no dad ever looked so fucking gleeful to have his house full of noise and kids. Weird, right?

So, I put it out of my head. The band grumbles something about one more song and then freight-trains away. The pit starts to churn again, and Scoops, he flickers.

SE: Flickers?

JM: That's the best way to describe it. Like, I saw the wall behind him and then he was back before I could blink. And… I don't know. There were a couple of dingy bulbs dangling overhead and they flashed at the same time. Made me think I was imagining all of it.

SE: What'd you think of that?

JM: Truth? That I got hit in the head harder than I first thought. What are you writing?

SE: You just gave us a suspect. Eye color, hair color, height, build, any of that?

JM: Normal.

SE: That's not really a description, kid.

JM: And yet. Sorry, man. Except for the outdated threads, you could've plucked this dude from any nine to five in the country. Height? Normal. Build? Normal. Eyes? It was dark and he was on the other side of the room. Hair? Dude wore a silly hat.

SE: Normal.

JM: Telling you, though. What you really want to write down is what happened next.

* * *

From the field notes of Officer Jessica Keeley:

I stood at the base of the stairs for twenty, thirty seconds, panning my flashlight around the room, searching for any sign of life. Nothing. "We need lights," I called. "Overheads, preferably."

The basement lights came on with a SHUMP, like someone slamming a pickaxe into a metal floor.

My gorge rose, and I couldn't speak for a minute. Any attempt at words would've made me vomit and contaminate the crime scene.

The makeshift stage drew my attention first. Atop it, a ragged cut of meat slumped over the drumset, sticks still in hand, like the drummer had used them to fend off an attack. Unsuccessfully. Around the drums, four more bodies, sliced to ribbons. Two guitarists, a bassist, and the corpse closest to the audience clutching a microphone in its butchered hand. The soft sizzle of feedback still whined from the mouths of the amplifiers.

Then there was the crowd. At first, I thought there were at least twenty people on the floor. Then I swept the room again, noting all the detached parts. An arm neatly severed just above the elbow. Someone's foot still inside a red Converse sneaker, but tattered off at the ankle. Maybe the shoe wasn't always red. A torso chopped in half, pelvis and chest loosely connected by a string of guts, so rubbery they appeared fake.

On and on and on and on.

I scrambled to a corner behind the stairs to vomit.

When my stomach settled as much as it was going to, I sidled up next to Officers Pendleton and Matranga, staring out over the wreckage.

"You see it?" whispered Matranga.

Movement. Something alive.

* * *

August 15th, 1999 - Interview with suspect Jake McKenzie. Conducted by Detective Steve Everard, continued.

SE: What happened next?

JM: …

SE: Jake, come on.

JM: I'm thinking, alright? Okay, okay, okay. I'm just gonna say it. You're gonna want to interrupt, maybe roll your eyes.

Just know, if you do? I fucking quit. Shit, yesterday I had to take a pre-calculus quiz. Logic, logic, logic. Numbers. Things that click into place and make sense. Now? Fuck, I'm…"

SE: Take your time.

JM: …

JM: So, Scoops—

SE: We're sticking with calling him Scoops, then?

JM: Don't interrupt! Shit! H-he flickered, and I thought it was my eyes playing tricks on me. Maybe the lights. Except, it was like they were working at the same… I don't know… rate?

Even the feedback seemed to pulse in time with his flickering. Then I started watching the crowd around him, and there's this girl, from my pre-cal class, actually. Amy. Nice chick, looks good in a tight MXPX shirt. Amy lets out this holler. Can't hear it over the band, but you sort of can, even if it's just in your head.

Then she vanishes.

Not like disappears, more like someone grabbed her ankles and dragged her to the floor. That part of the basement is relatively calm, so I watch to see if she gets back up.

She doesn't.

Something makes me look toward Scoops again.

He's still in the same position as before, but now that grin on his face? It's stretched wider. Dude's not just happy, he's downright ecstatic. It's weird, and it makes my stomach ache a little. Smiling's not a crime, though. The band wraps their last excuse for a song and wanders off stage, joining the crowd.

I scan the audience while the headliner sets up, looking for Amy. Detective, I'm telling you, I really expected her to pop up behind me with a drink in hand, the smell of a clove cigarette clinging to her because she just went outside for a smoke.

SE: But you didn't see her again.

JM: But I didn't see her again.

SE: Amy Collins. That right?

JM: How— You found her?

SE: …

SE: Parents called the station when she didn't come home. I'm sorry, kid. I probably shouldn't have said anything. Go on.

JM: Go on? Like it's that fucking easy? Jesus Christ. I mean, I know what I saw, but like, I still had this hope, and you just… God, fuck you, man.

SE: …

JM: I— Okay, okay. Last band is ready to play. Group called Thursday. Not bad. A little more melody than the other ones. Not that I could enjoy it, because that guy was still grinning. Ear to ear. Only he doesn't look happy anymore. There's something like hate in his eyes.

SE: Was he looking at you?

JM: Uh-uh. I think if I'd caught his gaze, I probably would've turned and run up the stairs, down the street, knocked over anyone who got in my way. Anyway, Thursday plays on. These clean-picked emo numbers that scream into some vicious breakdowns and get the pit swirling again. Only this time, I don't want anything to do with it. I don't want to take my eyes off Scoops.

So I press against the wall, splitting up a couple of half-in-the-bag headbangers who stare at me all worried-like. I don't know. Maybe I looked like I saw a ghost. Then he starts flickering again, and I scan the crowd because I'm shit-scared that I know exactly what's going to happen.

Long-haired guy in a Smashing Pumpkins shirt goes down first. I see him in the crowd and fucking BOOM! He vanishes out of sight, like the floor swallowed him, then others start disappearing. Faster and faster. Like, I can't even make out these people's features before a head gets sucked into the tide of bodies, an arm waves, throwing a drink up and making it rain.

Flicker flicker fucking fade, and Scoops is always back and Jesus fucking Christ, that smile. It just keeps getting wider.

SE: Slow down, kid.

JM: Fuck you, slow down. You didn't see it. You have no idea what it was like. By the time the fifth person dropped off the face of the earth, my heart was pounding in my chest like it was planning a prison break, trying make a clean getaway. And the corners of the guy's lips? Try and smile as big as you fucking can. Do it!

SE: ...

JM: No? Fine. Look. Look at this! Corners of my lips don't go up past my nose, they can't. It's not physically possible. So, tell me, how could it be that this guy's smile kept going, like... like an earthquake tearing cracks down the center of a street.

Jagged and crawling. To his ear lobes. Flicker. Top of his cheeks. Flicker. Up to his eyes, tearing his face apart. And every time you think it can't go any higher, another kid gets sucked into the pit and doesn't get up again, and it climbs.

SE: *clears throat* Look Jake, whatever you saw, it was traumatic. Sometimes the mind stretches to try to explain things. I've seen it a million times. It's like self-preservation.

JM: Don't patronize me. Don't. I know what I saw.

SE: Okay, I don't mean to condescend. Go on.

JM: …

JM: I think it was four songs into the set, something like that. The singer from Thursday's all out of breath. Skinny guy with a bowl cut, hair plastered across his face. He says, 'This next song's called "Dying in New Brunswick."'

It's about one of the worst days I ever had.' Slow, almost acoustic-style introduction, primed to build to something bigger. It never got to that peak, though. It was during that song that people noticed the bodies on the floor.

* * *

From the field notes of Officer Jessica Keeley:

Just a slight shift at first.

"When a soul leaves a body," whispered Matranga, "the electricity and the life don't always follow immediately." Twitches and spasms are commonplace among the recently deceased, but we eased over anyway, just in case.

Again, this next part won't make the final report. I need to get it down, though. My family used to vacation by the shore, Asbury Park, and I remember when you got down close to the water, the wet sand would suck at your bare feet and make a sound like slurping soup. The sluice of gore in that basement made a noise way too similar for comfort as we crossed the room.

Beneath the pile of bodies, that movement became more frantic.

Pendleton radioed in, said we might have a live one and to prep some paramedics. Despite the squelching and the tacky blood clinging to our shoes, we raced over and started combing through the meat, the shreds of clothing, until we unearthed a person gasping for air. A man. Boy? Who knew? Dark hair matted to his head and terror deep in his eyes. The kind you don't get over. The kind that requires therapy twice a week for the rest of your life. That primal appearance of trauma obscured his age. Blood soaked his clothes and his skin, though he appeared uninjured. Matranga tugged the guy to his feet and draped his arm over her shoulder, then helped him toward the stairs. The survivor said nothing, only let out ragged breaths like he was choking on smoke. As they started upstairs, I surveyed the room. No more movement. Not a spasm, not a twitch. An absolute wasteland.

The thump of footsteps halfway up the steps paused suddenly, and a raspy voice that left no illusion of youth trickled down into the basement. "Has anyone seen my hat?"

* * *

August 15th, 1999 - Interview with suspect Jake McKenzie. Conducted by Detective Steve Everard, continued.

JM: I'm not sure where the first shriek came from, but it spread like a virus. Then the door slammed shut at the top of the stairs. Screams, banging from both sides. I know how it sounds.

SE: We rounded up seven people from upstairs. We're still trying to figure out what happened on that floor.

JM: And I bet they all say the door closed by itself, didn't they? And then they couldn't get it open.

SE: ...

JM: I get that my story's a hard pill to swallow, but at some point, you're going to have to choke it down. You must've heard descriptions of the scene. Nothing natural about that. God, man, that panic didn't start because someone saw a friend on the floor, looked like they were taking a nap. That girl Amy, Smashing Pumpkins guy, all the others, they were fucking shredded. Like something with the power and sharp edges of a harvester plowed through that basement.

When the panic started, it was like the mosh pit became a living, breathing entity, taking up the whole room as people started dropping. More than before, faster than before. Scoops flickered, flickered, his smile reaching up like it was going to tip his hat. Another head disappeared, a sharp scream, someone else dragged underneath the trampling feet. And the smell? Shit, blood. They say it's got a metallic smell, and man, I wish I could've gone the rest of my life without knowing there's no better way to describe it.

SE: But you got out? The door slammed shut at the top of the stairs, immovable by all accounts, but you got out.

JM: The window. The basement had turned into this maelstrom, but since Scoops caught my attention, I'd been making my way to the outside of the crowd, of the room, where it was safest. All the kids still drawing breath? They funneled into the middle, towards the stairs. Ducks at a shooting gallery.

Meanwhile, Scoops flickered like morse code while the lights overhead kept time with him and the amplifiers shrieked. More bodies hit the floor. I hoisted myself and knocked out the glass. You see the windows? Nah, but you've seen the type. Barely big enough for a cat to slip through, and that's when there's no jagged edges, no broken glass, but I climbed and gave it my damnedest. The shards cut into me, and I pushed through the pain, popping out onto the street like a newborn calf, not far enough away to escape the screams.

SE: What did you use to break the glass?

JM: What? I don't know. My hands.

SE: Okay. Then you ran.

JM: I wish I had. No, I did the thing you're never supposed

to do. I looked back. And Scoops, he finally saw me. Still smiling, the corners of his lips reaching up past his fiery eyes, as he skipped like a scratched CD.

This is gonna sound crazy, I know, but I felt like if his grin grew any more, his face would peel back and reveal whatever lived underneath.

SE: *whisper* Christ, kid. What else did you see?

JM: Only a few bodies remained standing, and I could see gashes opening on their skin, limbs being torn off and thrown to the floor. I could hear them hit. Something attacking them, ripping them to pieces. Just doing it too fast to really see. And maybe that's the worst part. A killer on the loose and he can cut your throat before you see him make a move. That's when I ran, Detective.

SE: And where did you go?

JM: I started down Union—

SE: Toward your house?

JM: I guess. I just wanted to get somewhere safe. The road was empty and every time my feet slapped the asphalt it was like I could still feel that motherfucker watching, smiling, blocks away from the basement. Like his influence extended over the city, paved the streets with hate. I can almost feel it even here. At some point I must've stopped at a payphone to call for help.

SE: Hm. And that's all?

JM: …

JM: I'd really like a cigarette.

SE: *short, sharp laughter* It's a hell of a story, and I'm torn, kid. I really am. Because just about everything you told us lines up with the description of the crime scene, Officer Keeley's report. A bloodbath with no weapons left at the scene and no logical explanation. No natural explanation.

JM: So, what are you torn about?

SE: Well, it completely contradicts the story of the other survivor.

JM: The people upstairs? They can verify the door, but they didn't see anything in the basement. That's—

SE: No, kid, the other person we found alive in the basement. Pulled him out and brought him here. He was an even bigger mess than you. You had some scratches, a few from the glass, sure, but others… I don't know. Looked like defensive wounds to me. But this guy was doused in blood.

So, we cleaned him up and interviewed him first thing this morning. I can't give his name out or anything, but he owns the house. Said he was down in the basement, just making sure everybody was being safe. That some kid locked the basement door, pulled a machete, and just started swinging with… how'd he put it? 'Reckless abandon.'

JM: No. That's not— An older guy? From the basement? It's got to be him. Christ, what are you doing? Go track him down, arrest his ass!

SE: He's still in the building. Ready to take a look at you as soon as we're finished here, and— What're you looking at, kid? The lights? Don't mind them. It's an old station. Sometimes they flicker.

Liz Kerin

DOWN BY THE WATER

Liz Kerin

I was very careful not to tell you that you were ugly.

The topic of beauty was reserved for the inanimate, or the intangible. Our cottage was beautiful. The pearls we collected on the beach were beautiful. The Saints were beautiful.

My mother wove a tapestry for you, and we hung it above your cradle. You'd totter upright and trace each of the Saints' faces, interlaced with shimmering silver fibers. Their lithe, opalescent bodies, sinuous and mesmerizing. Gossamer fins that matched their gleaming hair. Yes, the Saints were beautiful. And we were allowed to say so. We could not compete with them, mere humans that we were. Putting them on a pedestal was tradition, a part of the world you were born into.

I taught you skills that would befit your bland appearance and give you an advantage. Knot tying. Sailing. Medicinal herbology. You would not be sent to the mainland as a bride when you came of age. But you'd be all right. When the other girls were learning to dance and speak foreign tongues, I kept you at home and taught you to gut herring. There was no reason to get your hopes up. I protected you—not from the truth, but from a life of heartache.

I was a good mother.

What became of you had nothing to do with me.

* * *

When your cousin Veronique was born, all the neighbors said she was "kissed by the sea." Our family could trace its heritage back to the year the Saints were devoured by the ocean and became the gods they are today, and we had always maintained a glimmer of hope that we shared a drop of their blood. Each time a new child came into the family, those rumors reignited. And Veronique's beauty certainly gave them credence.

She was two years younger than you, and she followed you wherever you went. She was shy, uncomplicated, and a fast learner.

I didn't want the two of you to be friends.

I knew what would happen when you discovered how different the two of you were; that *she* was meant for something more. But you were stubborn and relentless. You relished the warmth of her light. The attention you received when the two of you went out to collect pearls together. When I tried to keep you at home, you'd screech like a gull with its throat slit till I let you out. I wish you hadn't made it so difficult. I was only trying to help you.

The mainland had been courting Veronique for years. She became engaged on her sixteenth birthday, and the village threw her a gorgeous farewell feast. I told you not to drink too much. I knew you were emotional, and that the liquor would only make it worse. But you didn't listen. You confronted me between courses and asked why I never petitioned to have you go to the mainland. Why didn't you take the same courses as Veronique, or wear the same clothes? The two of you had lived parallel lives when you were young, but then something shifted. I begged you to drop the subject, but you refused. You started screeching like that blood-soaked gull again, in front of everyone. But even then, as fury seethed inside me like hot tar. . . I didn't tell you the truth. I delivered the same response, over and over: "You and your cousin have different talents, and so, you will live different lives." You poured yourself another glass of summer wine and stormed out to the docks to watch the fireworks. Alone.

At least, that's what I assumed.

But you weren't alone.

I know that, now.

Two days later, you skipped home from work on the docks—yes, skipped—and whirled into your seat at the dinner table, all smiles. I was struck by your sunny attitude. What had changed? You'd been morosely dragging your feet since the night Veronique left the island. When I served supper—warm bread, mussels, and a sweet lemon curd, you reported that you'd already eaten, and you weren't hungry.

"Who did you have dinner with?" I asked.

"A new friend." You couldn't hold still, twisting like a cyclone on your wooden stool. Twirling your stiff, salty hair around your finger over and over. You giggled as the color rose in your cheeks.

"A boy?" I arched a brow. You laughed even harder.

"Boys," you spat, like the word was rotten. "By summer's end, I'll never need to worry about boys again. Or any of you worthless bottom-feeders."

"Alize!" My mouth hung agape. "You watch your tongue at my table."

You shut up, then, but your sneer was like a splinter under my skin.

As you watched me eat, you produced a palm-sized ammonite from your pocket and started spinning it like a coin on your empty plate. I couldn't help but notice what a lovely specimen it was. So many of the fossils we'd collected on the beach were chipped and decaying, but this one was a sleek, shiny copper color consisting of three perfect, symmetrical spirals.

"That's beautiful," I remarked of the petrified shell, hoping to loosen the tension. "Where did you find it? If you take it to the jeweler, he might buy it for a fine price."

Your eyes shone like daggers as you protectively shoved the ammonite back into your pocket.

"And what would I do with the money?" You asked with an icy laugh. "Put it toward my dowry?"

As you held my stare, I couldn't help but notice the peculiar copper ring pulsing around your slate blue irises. The watery whites of your eyes were jaundiced and yellow.

"Alize, what did you have for supper tonight?"

You stood from the table without answering and sashayed off to your room.

The waves pummeled the cliffs in the sudden silence, like the drums of approaching war.

* * *

The following day, suppertime was the same. You weren't interested in eating, overcome by that same restless fidgeting.

"You've got to have *something*," I insisted much less patiently than the previous night. "Eat two prawns in front of me. Now."

That copper ring around your irises glistened in the lamplight. "You don't understand. My body already has the power to sustain me, all on its own."

"That's nonsense. You're going to start fainting at work and you'll fall off the boat if you don't eat."

You laughed. "You've always been such a simple woman, Maman. No imagination." You produced the ammonite from your pocket again and started spinning it on the table, just like you had the night before. When I studied it, it looked as though it had started to change color; a jewel-green pallor was creeping along the outer edges. But you snapped it up into your fist before I could get a closer look.

The next morning, while you were outside in the shower, I sifted through the dirty clothes on your bedroom floor till I found the linen skirt you'd been wearing the night before. The ammonite was still in your pocket, as I'd hoped.

I'd been right about its changing color. Half the outer ring was now green and, even stranger, the fossil was scalding hot to the touch, like a smoldering coal.

I dropped it on the floor with a gasp.

It hadn't seemed hot when *you'd* held it.

I continued interrogating its color and shape from a distance, until I noticed an etching on the innermost concentric ring.

A.L.

My heart catapulted toward my throat at the sight of the inscription. I knew, then, where you'd gotten it. . . and who had been advising you.

I marched outside to the shower and outhouse. The water wasn't running anymore, so I knew you could hear me when I banged on the flimsy driftwood door.

"Alize! Come out right now!"

You did not answer.

"I know you've been to see Amara Lune. I know what this is." My voice grew teeth.

Still, you didn't respond.

I kicked the door with a grunt, and the wood gave way against my heavy boot. I hadn't expected that, though maybe I'd hoped for it. The outdoor stall was cheaply built, like everything else your vile father added to the house before he deserted us for the damned Navy.

The shower was off, but the ground was still drenched. Not with water, though.

A foul stench hung in the humid air, so thick you could slice it like bread: Hot, salted sickness, as if the sea had boiled all of its inhabitants to death and sent them to the surface, squirming and shrieking, necrotic tentacles snarled in a panic.

You were naked, on your hands and knees, retching.

I gagged and yanked my collar up over my nose, afraid I'd collapse to the floor right beside you. I side-stepped the hideous tide of frothy bile you'd vomited, trying to get a closer look at your face. I realized then that it was more than just your sickness all over the floor; It was every repugnant humor your body could possibly excrete. Tributaries of blood wove through the stagnant, yellow-brown mire. Your weak, desiccated body convulsed as another wave erupted from every vulnerable part of you, and terror strangled my lungs as I dry heaved into my blouse.

I thought you would die if I didn't help you off the floor and force you to drink something. And that's what I was trying to do when I realized you'd already begun.

Sickened tears rose in my eyes, bidden by that horrible guzzling sound. Your gasps between gulps of septic filth.

"Alize. . ." My voice staggered. "Stop. We'll make this okay. *You'll* be okay."

You glanced up at me, but only for a second—the same way you'd glance at your own image in the mirror. Lightning fast and full of shame.

Trancelike, you returned to your task.

I remembered what you'd said the night before: *"My body already has the power to sustain me, all on its own."*

I should have known those weren't your words. Someone had taught you a mantra.

A spell.

I ran across the yard, leaving you in the shed to devour the abhorrent mess you'd made. I hated it, but I knew I couldn't save you on my own. Not if this was the work of that nefarious crone and her black magic.

I sprinted up the shoreline, to the place where the soft, downy dunes gave way to sharp granite cliffs, littered with whale bones and the shards of shipwrecks past.

When my friends and I were children, we would dare each other to sneak up the crumbling spiral staircase carved into the rock, slick with algae, to steal a "cursed" whale bone or baleen frond from among the rocks. What we didn't know, back then, was that there had never been a curse upon "Humpback's Tomb." It was the people who lived there that were cursed.

Amara Lune's family were outcasts: generations of traitors, descended from the Saints, who had defied their holy order by choosing a life on land. Over the centuries that followed, their bloodlines had been tainted by criminals, drunks, and other ne'er do wells who fled to Humpback's

Tomb to dodge the law. But Amara Lune had always kept her side of the street clean. Her family line had remained pure in the unspeakable way that cursed families often do. As such, her magic was real. But it came with a price.

A price I myself had paid eighteen years ago.

Your father was a handsome foreigner with a silver tongue who'd made me mad with a desire to burn down my life. A month before I was to be engaged on the mainland, I let him ruin me. He was not a 'good' man, by the village's standards. He committed petty crimes to stay afloat, then borrowed coin he couldn't repay to get out of jail. I was his ideal plaything: young, bored, and desperate to devastate my strict parents. Night after night, as he filled my cup, I'd say to myself, "You have no proof your future husband is a 'good' man, either. Better to find someone you love and create your own 'good' man."

I was sure having a child would shore us up. That the village would forgive my behavior once they saw the kind, loving father he would most certainly become. I didn't even mind that I'd have to stay on the island. This was the life I wanted. . . until I discovered I'd be living it alone. He was already making plans to move along.

But Amara Lune had the power to stop life in its tracks. All the girls in the village knew about the tinctures she'd sell. The benedictions she'd whisper in the dead of night, up on Humpback's Tomb. Nobody else knew about you, at that point. I could buy myself a fresh start. I could still go to the mainland.

I stole the money from him—money he'd intended to use abandon me—and I scaled the staircase to see Amara Lune that very night. But once I got home, I was too scared to drink the tincture she'd given me.

Within a few days, he was groveling at my door. He could no longer afford to leave town because of the money I'd stolen. I smiled knowingly, took him back, and threw the tincture into the sea.

Years later, after he'd finally left for good, you and I ran into Amara Lune in the marketplace one afternoon. She remarked how you must have "Deeply wished to live," and that you were destined for great things. I'd almost laughed in her face and told her the truth about the tincture, but I didn't want to risk escalating the topic. You might have heard something you were never supposed to hear. You might have discovered how close I'd come to ending your life.

So, all I said was, "Thank you, that's a very kind blessing," then I hustled you back home without finishing our errands.

I reached the top of Humpback's Tomb, panting, and Amara Lune opened the door to her cobblestone cottage with a smirk. Like she'd been expecting me. Every time I saw her—which wasn't often—I was struck by her unchanged appearance. Year after year, she was the same: haggard, yet ageless. Brown teeth like a weatherbeaten wooden fence, set behind plump, rosy lips and youthful dimples. Her skin was like glass—shatterproof and pearlescent. But it was her hair that was the most peculiar. All of it had fallen out except for a downy patch of white at the top of her skull, where she'd been struck by lightning during a hurricane as a young woman. Grotesque, pink scars in jagged, fern-like patterns spread from the top of her head down her neck and shoulders. The strange tessellations were beautiful in that unsettling, numinous way—like the perfect symmetry of a gutted creature's entrails. It was hard to look at anything else.

"Sweet Celine," she addressed me, wooden fence teeth on full display as she smiled. "To what do I owe the pleasure?"

"I think you know."

"Why don't you come inside, dear?"

I shuddered. I'd only been in Amara Lune's abode the once, and I had never wanted to go back. Fetal rats in jars flickered in my mind's eye. I remembered the massive decomposing squid that had been laid out on the kitchen table, being harvested for its long-dead ink. The smell of it.

"I'm fine where I am, thank you. And don't call me 'dear.' I'm not a child anymore."

"Fair." She narrowed her glaucous eyes. "But before you chastise me and demand I set your daughter free, remember: *she is a survivor.* Years ago, she showed you that she desired a full life. I am helping to facilitate that desire and make it a reality."

I sneered in response. A gust of unseasonably frigid air raked my spine. "She *survived* because I never took your damned tincture."

I was expecting Amara Lune to snicker in response. To call me weak and pathetic. Instead, her expression blackened. "Then what you have done is doubly cruel. You chose life for her, then you *snatched it away.*"

"I beg your pardon?"

"You taught her she was destined to fail because of the way she looked, did you not? You said society would judge her unfairly. But *you* were the first one to do that. *You* held her back. You didn't even let her try to improve her station. She could have become so much more."

"I was protecting her!"

"Come now, dear. That's nonsense. You just couldn't bear to see her succeed where you failed, could you?"

My head spun. This couldn't be true. Everything I'd done, I did in the name of sparing your feelings. How *dare* this woman accuse me of causing your discontent. Your self-hatred.

"When I saw your daughter's distress on the night of her cousin's engagement, I knew I had to intervene," Amara Lune went on. "But I didn't push her. I simply offered to sit and listen to her. The next day, *she* came to see *me.*"

"Well, whatever you gave her when she came to see you, it's killing her. She's half-conscious in a pile of her own filth. She's. . . she's—" I couldn't bear to repeat what I'd seen. But the witch already knew.

"She's sustaining herself and discovering her true power," Amara Lune offered, again with that know-it-all smirk. "I've given her the ammonite to keep track of the time and to stay strong. And she *will* be strong. She wants this. More than anyone who's ever come to my door."

"Wants *what*? What in God's name are you doing to her?"

"I am blessing her with her the beauty of the Saints, and the opportunity to join them."

My jaw hung loose. My voice felt like cobwebs in my throat.

"B-but the Saints aren't—"

"Aren't real?" She chuckled. "You'd dare speak such blasphemy?"

"She can't just *join them*. They live under the sea. They're thousands of years old!"

The crone shrugged. Twisted scars undulating in time with her cold laughter.

"Your daughter *did* say you had no imagination."

"Undo this. Immediately. Or I'll have the priests evict you and throw you in jail."

"I cannot undo it. She's already taken my magic into her body. Once she's swallowed the extract, it's out of my hands. Plus," she added slyly. "My records are impeccable. The law has no power over me. I don't let anybody undergo treatment without written consent. Surely, you must remember."

My gaze dropped to my feet. How could I forget? I, too, had signed a contract the night I visited her. Stamped the parchment with a drop of my blood.

"The best thing you can do is encourage her," Amara Lune filled the silence. "Better late than never, right?"

I shuffled back toward the crumbling staircase, face burning. Eyes still pinned to the ground. A scream throbbed in my chest, but I didn't let it out till I was back on the beach. The gulls squawked in reply, as though that smug old bitch had sent them to laugh at me.

* * *

When I returned home, the outhouse was clean. I didn't want to ask how you'd accomplished that.

I couldn't bring myself to encourage you. But maybe, if I were kind, gentle, and helpful when you were sick, you'd lose your resolve to defy me. Maybe you'd stop "sustaining" yourself and your body would heal on its own.

That night, I asked you to explain the ammonite to me. I kept my face and tone neutral. Simply allowed you to speak.

You'd been hesitant at first, but eventually held the stone out for me to see.

"The entire journey takes nine days," you said, showing me the bottle-green band that had already formed along the outermost spiral. "Each spiral marks three days. Each day, there's a new change. See?" You leaned in close, pulling your lower eyelid down to show me the whole of your iris.

It was completely copper. No trace of blue remained.

You grinned.

"It's starting."

Did the Saints have copper eyes? I couldn't be sure. Nobody had seen them for over a thousand years. . .

The next day, you "sustained" yourself again when the sun rose. I cried in bed, holding a pillow over my ears to drown out your retching.

That night, you started picking your skin beside the fire, staring into the flames with an entranced kind of vacancy. When I came to send you off to bed, I stifled a shrill gasp as my mouth filled with the silvery taste of terror. You were pulling a long, flaccid strip of flesh from your cuticle all the way down to your elbow crease, exposing viscous green pillows of poisoned muscle underneath. You threw your shed skin onto the fire, then started on a new section. When you noticed me standing there, you held up your butchered arm and whispered, "Isn't it beautiful, Maman?"

The savory smell of burnt flesh filled the air between us.

I ran outside and hurled my supper into the sand.

"Doesn't it hurt?" I whispered to you the next day as you lay in bed, struggling to breathe. Shredded skin hung like rags all around you. I could see bone protruding from the glutinous green sinew that was once your knee. "You can't tell me you're not in pain. You can make this stop, you know. You have that power."

"It doesn't hurt." You shuddered as you spoke, breath rattling in and out.

"You can barely breathe!" I raised my voice for the first time in days.

"That's the point, Maman. Air doesn't suit me anymore. Soon I'll be able to breathe underwater. And then it will be time."

My heart sank as I glanced at the ammonite on your bedside table. Only a small shred of its original color remained. The green spiral was nearly complete.

"You can be whatever you want, without all this," I whispered, a desperate twinge in my voice. "I never meant to make you feel like you had no future. Whatever your dream is, I swear I'll dedicate my life to helping you pursue it."

You wheezed, unshed tears in your eerie copper eyes. "My dream is *this*."

You reached for my hand. I hated myself for recoiling.

"And you *are* helping, Maman. Thank you."

* * *

On the ninth day, I rose before the sun and took a seat beside your bed. Your whole body was a sickly olive green, fragile as wet paper. Maybe you were meant to leave this world. To join the Saints. Maybe I'd been wrong all along. About everything.

I watched the labored, infrequent rise and fall of your chest. I'd been waiting to see if something resembling gills might form. Then, I'd know for sure that this was real. Then, I'd escort you to the water so you could realize your dream. But no sooner.

Your eyes fluttered open, and you started pawing at your grotesquely exposed ribcage, no doubt trying to locate the same features I'd been searching for.

"How are you feeling, dear?" I murmured in a voice cramped with emotion. I knew what'd you say, though. The same thing you'd said yesterday:

"Ready." What remained of your lips curled back, exposing your loose teeth. I realized you were trying to smile. "Will you take me to the dock at sundown?"

Every part of me wanted to scream, No. A thousand times, no. But if your body couldn't withstand the air anymore. . . if you would truly become one of *them* by day's end. . .

"If you're confident you'll be able to breathe, then yes," I choked out. You closed your eyes with a contended half-nod, and I stayed seated at your bedside, watching stripes of sunlight stretch across your hollow, decaying face.

For the past day and a half, I'd been too afraid to let myself rest. I couldn't so much as blink without a rush of fear that I'd lose yet another precious moment with you. And yet, I was powerless to control my body's reflexes, just like you.

Hours later, I awoke in the same spot. Blades of shadow portioned the room. I had no idea how long I'd been asleep. All I knew was that I was alone.

You had disappeared from your bed.

I swept through the kitchen, incandescent with panic, calling your name.

The house was still. The only sound was the clatter of hanging pans as my feet pounded past the stove.

There was no sign of you. . . except for the bloodstained butcher knife lying on the cutting block. I swallowed a squall of tears as I followed the angry trail of thick, clotted blood to the front door. You'd stepped in some of the mess, leaving a trail of footprints that showed the strange, deformed shape of your rotting feet. I bolted out onto the beach, bathed in dusky golden light.

Pearl-hunting hour.

Our favorite time of day.

I screeched your name, over and over, as I followed the blood across the sand. The tide was rising and starting to wash your trail away, but I spotted you wading in the water, fighting to hold yourself upright. As I raced toward you, splashing madly, eyes ablaze with salt, I noticed the blood dripping down your rail-thin, decomposing hips.

You'd slashed yourself three times on both sides of your body.

"Alize, stop! Come home with me!" I called out to you in anguish.

"Maman, it's time. I'm ready," you whispered. Barely audible over the crash of the waves.

"No, you're *not* ready! Look what you've done to yourself!"

You managed one last spectral, toothless smile as you sank to your knees. "Yes. I'm beautiful now."

A massive, vengeful wave churned on the horizon. You greeted it with open arms.

"Alize! NO!"

As the wave crashed over you, I leaped forward and snagged you in my arms, desperate to keep the sea from consuming you. The ferocious undertow dragged us out and under, and I felt you start coming to pieces. You slipped from my grasp, like your body was made of sand. I struggled to hang on, to grab a strand of your thin hair or braid my fingers with yours. . . but there was nothing to hold onto. You'd broken to bits. And the fish were already circling.

I knifed toward the surface and broke through with a ragged howl. Gulls swooped into the water, desecrating your final resting place. I treaded water and watched, helplessly catatonic, as nature devoured all that was left of you.

Once the last abominable scavenger had flown off, my leaden legs propelled me back toward the shore of their own volition. I'm not sure how I wound up back on the beach, paralyzed and shivering, as the sun sank beneath the sea to join you.

Look what you've done to yourself. My last words to you battered the inside of my skull.

You didn't do this alone, though. My stomach roiled, hungry for comeuppance.

But not against Amara Lune.

Suddenly, as though summoned by my treacherous thoughts, a bony hand clutched my shoulder, and the nefarious crone dropped a copper ammonite into my lap.

"Free of charge," she rasped in my ear. Her breath reeked of sweet salt and decomposing flesh. "Never say I wasn't merciful. There is always a way out."

"Give me my daughter," I said, in a hoarse, tattered voice.

I found the strength to whirl around and face her.

But Amara Lune was gone. She'd already slipped between the jagged shadows of Humpback's Tomb, looming up above like a storm.

I let out a breath and picked up the ammonite. It pulsed in the palm of my hand, greeting me with a wicked green wink. Gloating. Watching. Waiting.

Waiting to drag me beneath the waves where I belonged.

THE
PSYCHOGRAPHIST
a novel
CARSON WINTER

A SPECTRE
IS HAUNTING
GREENTREE
CARSON WINTER

&#?!

AVALINE TRIO
THE MENZI
ABSENT MINDS
PENSKE FILE
THROW
DEAD BARS
RAMONA
NO
PUNK ROCK
RUINED
MY LIFE

BASTARDS OF YOUNG

Carson Winter

VERSE

There were four of them that night. Young, scrawny, with muscles coiled like springs. Fists like sledgehammers, hair shorn to a stubble. No shirts, just ancient denim vests—re-stitched a dozen times with dental floss; stiff from decades of sweat, a hodgepodge of band patches, fabrics, bleach stains, zippers, and studs—all Frankenstein'd together by clumsy, illogical hands.

The band was playing loud, and I was on my second beer, standing in the back, watching with curiosity as these vicious looking kids swung wildly at each other, at bystanders, even at the fucking amps at the front of the stage. At one point, the doorman had to pull out his flashlight, plow through the pit, and grab one of the kids by his greasy lapel, giving him a warning, and then throwing him back into the frenzy of sweating, fighting bodies. When he walked away, I saw him wipe his hands on his jeans in disgust.

Alan was nodding his head, holding an arm out in front of himself, lest any careening bodies try to topple him into the bar.

I put my mouth to his ear. "Who are they?" I yelled.

"Who?"

The music buried every syllable in a coffin of fuzz. "The ones in the vests. Trying to start shit."

Alan shrugged. "Fuckin' kids. They're always around."

One band left the stage, and another took their place. Four on the floor beat, guitars that sounded like a swarm of hornets, a howling vocalist with his heart on his sleeve. Springsteen on methadone, loud but tuneful. The men and women in the front sang along, taking on the melody of the big chorus, shouting the words together, swaying back and forth.

But the kids were locked into a different rhythm. They punched and shoved each other; chaotic bodies out of time and place. The crowd around them grew uneasy— shaking their heads, pulling back, abandoning the singalong for the bar.

I could see them clearly as the crowd thinned, bouncing around with manic energy, their lips twisted in cruel sneers. One pulled his arm back and launched it—a sharp snap with surprising speed—that caught his cohort in the jaw. He was laughing, spitting teeth. Blood ran down his chin, black under the stage lights. One jumped onto the other, bending down to his earlobe, taking it between his teeth and yanking like a wildcat.

"Jesus Christ," said Alan.

Another elbow, another punch. A spinning kick that caught a woman in the throat. That was the one that did it. The music stopped.

"Hey! Bring the lights up!" yelled the frontman.

The venue was bathed in an orange glow. Two bouncers, big guys with an easy 600 pounds between them, ran into the pit and grabbed two kids each.

I heard one of the bouncers as he passed me. "If I ever see you fuckers again..."

Up close, they looked to be no more than eighteen. Perpetually rageful hellions. The one closest to me was missing half his ear—a bloody, jagged line of bright red pumped down into the collar of his denim vest.

Before they threw them out, I saw the writing on their backs.

BASTARDS, in a Friz Quadrata arc. Below it, a stenciled circle with a small X marking its outer line on the far left.

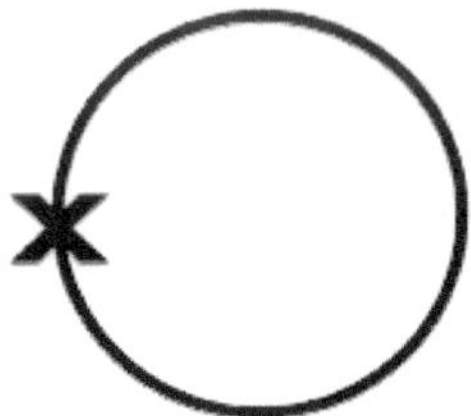

Alan said, "Just a local crew. A bunch of fucked up kids."

I nodded, still staring at the maniacal teens as the door closed. "The Bastards?" I asked.

"That's what they call themselves."

After a short apology, the band began to play again.

My mind was elsewhere.

CHORUS

Outside the venue, along the brick wall that faced the main throughway, men and women in flannel shirts and ripped jeans stood with subdued interest.

The smell of spray paint soured the summer night air.

Across the wall, painted in clumsy lettering:

USERS AND RUNAWAYS
WE ALL DIE THE SAME
LIVE LIKE MAYFLIES
BURN OUT IN FLAMES

VERSE

The next day, I found myself sitting outside my apartment building watching the light rail pass me by. I pulled out one smoke, lit it, burned it to a nub, then pulled out another. I closed my eyes and saw vicious smiles, crooked teeth, split lips; bodies on the verge of combustion.

I was new to the city. Mid-thirties, starting over after a bad breakup. She told me I wouldn't grow up, so I showed her how right she was. I moved to the city with big dreams—*Our Band Can Be Your Life* dreams. I wanted to be Michael Azerrad—the punk rock journalist, the insider, the dude who could tell you in a hundred thousand words that you just had to be there.

But I also knew that my knees hurt; that with my growing stomach, my old black Gildan tees didn't fit as well around the midsection. I traded in Vans for New Balances. Vic called it a mid-life crisis, wanting to be a part of this. I never said she was wrong.

I called up Alan—a college bud who took Frost's diverging road and ended up here, ungratefully living my dream in my stead. He picked up as I lit my third smoke.

"So, I was thinking," I said. "About last night."

"The Bastards," he said.

"I was thinking of doing a piece on them."

"Like an article?"

"Sure, yeah, an article."

Alan wrote for an online zine, and he had somehow turned that into the most minor celebrity status one could imagine. There was no money in it, but bands occasionally gave him their drink tickets and awkward, forced "Thanks" for covering their music.

"You write articles now?"

"I could. Why not?" I stood up, paced on the gray sidewalk, watched storm clouds gather weight overhead. A sweet breeze promised rain.

"I don't know, man. You just—you haven't written much."

"But I could. I did a couple of reviews. One of them got into Razorcake."

"Sure, yeah." The faintest hint of sarcasm. "Go for it," he said.

"I just want to get involved." I already felt myself floundering for validation. "Could be, like, a subcultural exploration. Local punk kids raising havoc. Drugs, violence, rock'n roll."

"Could be something," he said, coolly. "But these aren't kids you want to fuck around with."

"They're street kids. I've met street kids before."

"But you haven't heard the stories," he said. "I mean, you've been out of it for so long..."

Target bags, empty Gatorade bottles, and dead leaves formed a cyclone in the parking lot of my apartment building. The clouds flashed. Thunder exploded.

"Tell me, then."

I could hear the shrug in his voice. "It's just a rough scene." Subtext: *you wouldn't understand.* "Lots of drugs, lots of kids who don't make it out. One guy was telling me that, of all the kids he used to go to shows with in the 80s, not a single one survived."

I swallowed a pang of jealousy. "What about the Bastards, though?"

"The usual," he said. "Delinquents who like to cause a ruckus. Tale as old as time." He paused. "I remember hearing one thing, though. After they raised hell at this other show, a buddy of mine said he saw them going down into the sewer. Like, poppin' open a grate, see ya later."

"Really?"

"Really."

The image of the Bastards going underground made their mystique seem that much more delicious. "There's a community like that in Vegas," I said, perhaps too excitedly. "They live in storm drains. Beds, furniture, color TVs, the whole deal. Not a bad deal, if you ask me."

"Go to a show, maybe you'll see some," he said, maybe not warm to the idea that I was encroaching on his turf, but getting there. "Ask around. Be careful." The last part was an afterthought.

I found some canvas, some old white-out, a little needle and thread. For better or worse, I knew how to attract attention.

The storm clouds gathered strength as the sweet wind gathered speed. In the sewers, they probably had no idea.

* * *

I ignored a phone call from my ex, because there was nothing I could say that would make us work. I wasn't moving back, she wasn't taking me back. We were a memory, a schism, a handful of arguments, and nothing more. Just like when I was young, I turned to music to absolve me, to make me whole again. It's incredible what a song can do.

It was raining, so I took the light rail downtown. Outside, the buildings became dark and shiny and mysterious. It's funny how rain can do that. Such a simple thing, but it's transformative.

Still, I felt alone.

On the train: outcasts, weirdos, addicts, drunks; adolescents coming home after the ball game; college kids going out for a night of drinking and debauchery, excitedly predicting the night—how much they'd drink, who they'd fuck, which bar they'd hit first or last.

I envied them.

The show I was going to was nothing. A nowhere. No big headliner, no touring acts. Just local bands, mean-mugging, stomping, yelling, riffing, and bleeding on their nights off from their day jobs.

These types of shows were always a gamble. Sometimes there'd be this magnetic, diamond-in-the-rough energy. Sometimes there'd be a transparent veneer. Kids trying to act tough, failing in their cartoonish intensity. Sometimes they would have the charisma to carry you with them, sometimes they wouldn't. It was a coin toss.

I got off the train at the edge of downtown, where the shiny buildings became brick. Where the brewpubs became dive bars.

Sound check bled into the street as a crowd waited for entry on a dirty sidewalk. Thumping bass, heavy chords, cymbals crashing. I had downloaded a recording app on my phone, to feel like a real journalist. I daydreamed of sitting down with one or two of the Bastards, plying them with smokes or booze and getting them to talk to me outside. I imagined how they'd answer my questions—uneducated, but lucid, articulate; street-wise wisdom and youthful bravado boasted from the mouth of babes. The stuff that makes stories.

I searched the crowd around me. Maybe the Bastards didn't come for openers. Maybe they were drinking in the alley outside. Maybe they were in the city park a couple blocks away, or watching the bouncer carefully, waiting for him to turn his head so that they could rush the door and push in.

The possibilities only heightened my excitement, my vicarious delight.

I've always felt trapped by myself. Like there's always been another person inside me waiting to shake off the shackles of flesh and decorum; to burst forth from my body, a skeleton emerging from flesh and muscle; somehow more authentically myself than me. If not for a life, then at least for the duration of a song.

One band played and I rocked back and forth, slamming my false flesh against the false flesh around me. No booze, no drugs—clean and sober, a newborn. I caught my breath between sets, looking for backslaps and hugs from other catharsis-hungry miscreants. But no, they all had their own people. They disappeared from the front of the stage to smoke and to talk shit and to consider quietly leaving early.

Another band started a chainsaw storm of power chords and distortion, a whirlwind of sound and violence, machine-gun vocals rat-a-tat-tatting, ricocheting in my skull. Once again, I was locked in within everyone else, a school of fish, a community.

One person hit me.

I hit them back.

We both smiled as the band launched into another number.

More people flooded in, more of them found themselves at home around me, pressing into me, becoming me. They were all skeletons; they wanted a release from themselves too, to be boiled down to their authentic essence. A pile of vibrating bones, vibrating together.

My lungs were on fire. My eyes burned with salt and sweat. I was older than everyone else by at least ten years, which shouldn't have been a shock. But that's the thing about aging—you're constantly relearning your limitations.

At the back of the bar, I filled up a paper cup with lukewarm water and downed it. My ears were ringing. Everyone always told me I shouldn't stand so close to the stage. It was a health hazard. I was tired. Sore. I'd have bruises in the morning, and I knew I'd wake up and groan the first time I stood, railroad spikes shooting up through my heels. My head would throb.

I felt like a fool. A kid. I was an idiot. A pretender who never learned to let go. *Unable* to let go because I was too afraid to see what was next. Vic'd always tell me, "You're going to get old, you know? Don't you want a house? A yard? Savings? Kids? People around you?" And I'd shake my head and give what I thought was a devil-may-care smile—charming when you're twenty, stupid when you're thirty-five—and say, "All I want is a song."

I went outside. Rain fell, thunder roared. I lit a cigarette that extinguished nearly instantly. I turned the corner from the bar, into a brick alley.

I got my song.

CHORUS

Voices. Loud.

A loose, simple melody, given life by the exuberant.

The words echoed down the alley. I threw the cigarette to the side and followed.

USERS AND RUNAWAYS

WE ALL DIE THE SAME

LIVE LIKE MAYFLIES

BURN OUT IN FLAMES

VERSE

I ran down the alley. It was like a dream, almost. A perfect dream. You're always running in a dream. I turned out of the alley and, about three blocks away from me, I saw them.

There were four of them, same ratty vests, same shaved heads. Same circle and X on the backs of them, stitched with dental floss and dragged through time. I slowed down.

I walked to the end of one block, then another, then another, until I passed through a chain-link fence, cut open to allow access to the river. Shipping containers surrounded me.

The river was black. "Styxian," I said aloud, testing the word.

I wasn't expecting a response.

I followed the echoes of the Bastards' revelry as they moved across the riverfront, their voices bouncing off the towers of shipping containers. I stayed close to them and the sounds of their laughter—sharp and dangerous.

I peered around the edge of a container. The moon was out now, reflected in the wet surface of the asphalt. There they were. Four of them, just like the first night. They'd unearthed a couple of twelve packs of cheap beer from some hiding spot and were alternately draining them in a single pull, then throwing them full force at the ground, dancing in glee as the glass shattered.

Did I just walk out and say hi? Did I offer to buy them something? Weed? Beer? Coke? Seeing their lithe, tumble-dried bodies made me feel a world apart, and for a second I thought of leaving.

But then one of the Bastards turned to me and pointed.

He made a sound; not any words I could recognize, but instead some guttural bark. The other three turned too, their eyes wide and observant; curious and sharp. They moved as a group, cautious but unafraid.

"I saw you guys the other night," I said meekly. "At the show. I wanted to know more about you—the Bastards." I could barely get the sentence out. They weren't walking anymore. They were in a light jog. "I'm writing a story—"

One of them leapt into the air, arm cocked, fist the size of a pomegranate, and laid into me. All those cartoon cliches about seeing stars were proven firsthand. I wobbled, not quite hitting the ground, but slumped up against a container. My vision went out, my head throbbed, and I struggled to stand. I held out a hand, trying to tell them to stop, that I was a friend.

Another hit.

Probably a knee, right into my gut. The air emptied from my lungs and my hands went to my chest, trying to force the air back in somehow. Around me, there was a chorus of loud hollering—jeers. The hellions were both amused and emboldened by my pain, by my confusion. Kicks to my legs to send me hurtling the rest of the way to the earth, the rocky asphalt pushing its pebbles through my jeans and into my knees. More punches— one in my side, right to the kidney. Another Bastard boxed my ear.

I tried to fight back.

Fuck the story, I thought, but my punches were blind, unsure. I got my fist on one of them, but if it hurt, he didn't show it. He just laughed, let out another strange noise, then hit me back harder.

The hits only stopped when I stopped moving.

My eyes were swollen, my brain was bouncing against my inner skull, and I was certain that a rib was broken. Blood poured from abrasions all across my body.

One of the Bastards made another barking, coughing, hacking sound. Some call to action that I couldn't understand. I was about to open my mouth, to spit out the cracked half of a tooth, to ask, mouthing words around an exposed nerve, if they'd just talk to me, just tell me who they were, tell me a story.

But when I opened my eyes, just a squint, I saw their heads cocked quizzically. They were whispering to each other, questioning something, pointing at me—at the new patch I'd sewn on to my chest. A circle with an X along its outer rim.

The Bastards above me grinned.

I grinned too.

I thought they finally understood.

I got up, propping myself on the cold metal of the container. I'd taken my share of beatdowns before. My head swam with white lights, bright slashes that cut through my vision.

One more time.

"I just want to talk," I said, each word coming out like a gasping breath.

The Bastards grabbed my legs and began dragging me. I squirmed at first, kicked. But they took my kicks like they were gifts, then returned them tenfold, steel-toes parting my flesh and reverberating through my bones.

One of them propped open the entry to the sewer.

I heard its metal scrape across the concrete.

They pulled me over to the edge.

"Please, stop, don't," I muttered, unconvincingly. But even I knew the score by now. They didn't care, they weren't listening. They rolled me into the dark mouth of the sewer, and I fell twenty feet into a wet stream of waste. Something cracked, more air pushed from my lungs, pain everywhere. Exhausting hurt crashed like waves through my body.

Then, one by one, the Bastards came, jumping down beside me. Landing like cats. They dragged me further. Sewer water splashed into my eyes and mouth. I choked on it; vomit dribbled from my lips. But they kept me moving, deeper and deeper into the underground.

When they let me go, my eyes finally began to adjust.

Moonlight from a sewer grate filtered in from above me. It was just enough to make out my surroundings, the broad strokes at least. Graffiti covering the walls. Empty beer cans. Used needles. Blood spatter. The sewage flowed around my ankles. Across the way, I saw the snickering Bastards. Their faces pale in the moonlight, their eyes sunken and ringed with black.

"Tell me... tell me about yourselves," I managed to mutter.

But instead, those pale faces disappeared into the blackness. I heard their booted feet clang up a ladder.

I couldn't move. I was too tired. Age caught up with me, after all. Cold, alone, afraid.

But then the night went indigo, and I heard those boots again.

Those faces—forgotten kids, I assumed—appeared again from the dark and I braced for another beating.

Instead, they settled against the sewer walls, just like me. I saw them lay their heads back and open their mouths like venus flytraps, eyes rolling back into their skulls. I saw their skin shrivel into dried paper, then flake off the muscle, falling in dried jerky-like clumps into the stream.

Until they were nothing but bones, draped in a uniform.

Mayflies.

Bastards.

CHORUS

Each night they'd get up and do the same thing. They were agents of chaos, of youthful rage; boredom and violence. Whenever I worked up the energy to stand, to try to escape, they'd break a new bone. When I screamed for help, they'd slam my face into the cement. During the daylight, I watched their rotting bodies. At night, I watched them come alive again.

It's amazing what can be done in the length of a song. But as my body withered away, as the pain became so strong that I begged for death, I began to look forward to singing with them.

USERS AND RUNAWAYS

WE ALL DIE THE SAME

LIVE LIKE MAYFLIES

BURN OUT IN FLAMES

NOW
PUNK
&#!?
99
99
riley
PUNK
MUSIC

A BOX FULL OF SHARP OBJECTS

Shannon Riley

Replay it.

Close your eyes.

Pay attention.

You can hear her screams if you listen, I say, rewinding the track just right.

His face is inches from mine, we're close enough I can breathe him in. He smells a little stale, a little unwashed, but we both are. My bedroom is small, and the carpet hasn't been vacuumed all summer, but I dig my fingers into the fibers anyway and hold on so I don't float away. My other hand cradles a half-spent cigarette. He looks at me, and I can tell he hears her.

They say some freak chemical reaction caused the honey to melt all her flesh away, I explain, grabbing my phone to search for the image of the album cover art.

He asks me what kind of chemical reaction, angling the phone in his direction to see. The woman on the cover is nude, on her knees, and tilting her head back to receive long, sensual drips of golden honey into her mouth and down her body. Everything is shrouded in a 1970s haze, the colors warm and the edges soft, but the jar of honey in the model's hand is bright, as if it's the light source of the entire photograph.

Or an allergic reaction, or something, I'm not really sure, I say. But it ended her modeling career. And so, in a blind rage, she stormed into the recording studio while the band were tracking *Love Rollercoaster* and threatened to kill everyone.

His eyes are wide as he waits for the rest of the story. He licks his lips, and his tongue catches on the dry skin.

I continue.

My heart is beating so fast it hurts.

But when she started to get violent, the producer turned on her and stabbed her to death, I say. That's what you're hearing.

He asks me if that's true.

You hear the scream, don't you?

He sighs fuck on an exhale. He pops his earbud out and rolls over onto his back. I follow and raise the cigarette to my lips. We lie in silence, doing nothing but watching as the smoke drifts lazily up to disappear in the blades of the ceiling fan. My room is warm, and the curtains are drawn. The basement walls are covered with posters, relics of my fleeting interests, all sci-fi movies and pop punk bands, curling with age. Piles of unsorted laundry and books suffocate the surface of my dresser. A hair straightener.

The empty hamster cage. My book bag's somewhere. I never really cleaned it out at the end of the school year, so it's likely still tucked away, bloated with end-of-year bullshit I won't see again until August.

I pass the cigarette over, dropping the filter in between his lips so he can inhale.

He's oddly silent. I crane my neck up to see him. He's staring at the ceiling, the shared cigarette propped neatly in his mouth. His profile is so beautiful my stomach twists. He looks troubled, worried, and he wears the stress like a faded leather jacket.

Why would they keep her screams on the track? he mumbles, the cigarette bouncing between the syllables.

I roll from my back onto my side so I can curl myself around him. I press my nose into his soft cheek. I feel the heat of the cherry as he inhales again, and I imagine it sweetly singeing my skin.

They kept it as a souvenir, I say, my lips dancing across his skin. That way she'd be a part of them forever.

He swallows hard.

He says he thinks it's horrible.

Asks me if I agree.

I don't see it that way. No, she lives on like this, I say. Imagine getting to keep someone. No matter if they live or die or move away, they stay with you. They can always hear her, they can relive those last few seconds. All they have to do is spin a vinyl.

My skin tingles thinking about it and I sit up. He looks into my eyes and I lean close to him. Doesn't that sound romantic? I ask.

He smiles and pulls me down toward him. He tells me it sounds hot as fuck and his fingers start to roam. The interruption comes a minute later, the ringing of his phone, his mom telling him she's going to pick him up, that he needs to watch his little sister tonight. I roll my eyes and pretend to pin him down so he can't leave. His hands curl around my ribcage.

I wish I could keep you here with me all night, I laugh, twisting to avoid the tickles.

He tells me he wishes he could, too.

Something curious turns over in my head.

I want to keep a piece of you here with me, I tell him.

A piece of me, he repeats.

I ask him if he'd let me.

I watch him as the question lingers between us. His brows crinkle. He's trying to figure me out, but I'm already moving, stretching my body to reach for something under my bed. My fingers curl around the shape, wooden and rigid, and I drag it out over the dirty carpet. I place it in between me and him.

It's a box, about large enough for a pair of shoes to sit inside. The corners are worn, and scratches mar the otherwise smooth edges. It came from someplace unknowable, an attic or the basement or an uncle's garage. It doesn't really matter, all I know is that it came to die in the darkness below my mattress. My palm caresses the top panel. It's cool to the touch.

I ask him again, will he let me keep a piece of him here?

He sits up. Like what, he wonders.

What's something your mom won't notice?

His eyes haven't left the surface of the box.

He wants to know what's inside.

I tap my fingernails on the wood, gently, just for a moment, just long enough to see his shoulders tense. Then I wedge my nails under the lid and pry it open.

He asks me what that's all for.

I don't answer. Instead, I reach inside, letting my fingers drift along the slices of metal, the serrated edges, the cool handles, until I pull out a pair of scissors.

Come here, I say.

I tell him to just trust me, and he doesn't question me. He pushes closer in, rocking forward on his knees. His nose almost brushes mine and I feel the moist air of his breath on my skin.

Just some off the back, where no one will see, I tell him, sliding the scissors up toward the nape of his neck. I snip off a patch of hair. He barely winces. I can't help but run the blunt edges of the clippings along the dry skin of my lips, and then I tuck the bits of him away into the box.

Now I get to keep you, I tell him.

You're my *Love Rollercoaster.*

Outside, his mom honks her horn.

* * *

I feel warm knowing he's under my bed, tucked away in my little box, just a breath away each night. When I can't sleep, I reach down and let my fingers dance along the wooden surface until I finally go under. Throughout the week I check in on him. Just little peeks, maybe a little touch, or just to breathe him in or to count the coarse hairs. Having a little bit of him nearby is so good. But it's just not enough.

I pull the box out on Saturday night. My damp palms slide along the wood. I'm so nervous, but I'm tingling everywhere. I know it's a good idea, but I'm still afraid he'll say no. I ask him how it felt, being in my box this whole time.

It felt like I was with you all week, my boy says, eyes round with awe. I felt it. It wasn't a very strong feeling, but it was there.

I tell him I need more.

We need more.

I pluck his hand, hanging limply by his side, and I rest it on my thigh. I look carefully at each finger, run my thumb along his knuckles. I need one, I decide. I dive into my box. Metal scrapes against metal as I shuffle around for what I'm looking for. There it is, small and silver. I squeeze the hinge a few times, testing its resistance.

You want me to clip my nails? he asks.

I flip the clippers over and push out the thin metal file. I press it gently into the sensitive space beneath one of his nail beds. He doesn't flinch. I'm so proud of him, he's so good already. I tell him, no.

I need him to pry off one of his nails.

I need to have one.

It'll hurt, he says, plainly.

Good.

* * *

What a beautiful thing we have, something small and secret. During the week he sends me photos of his finger, wrapped tight in a flesh colored bandage. I ask to see what it looks like beneath, and he peels back the latex to show me. The tip of his finger, where the nail once was, is fleshy and angry red, puffy, weepy. I roll his nail, my gift, in my mouth and over my tongue as I scroll through the pictures in my phone gallery. The blue light from my phone shines in the dark. I'm inches away and my eyes sting from it. I lie back in my bed and balance my phone against a pillow so I don't have to take my eyes off the images. There's a throbbing between my legs, and my fingers inch just low enough to feel all shivery about it. I don't shut my eyes the entire time. My heart feverishly pumps my blood, desperate for it to reach everywhere all at the same time. I pinch the screen with my other hand, zooming in tight until the discolored, swollen nail bed is all I can see.

It looks painful.

It looks raw and sore and it's good it's good it's so good it's—

Fuck.

I end up closing my eyes at the very end after all. I spit the nail back out, a long string of saliva still connecting it to my lips.

I text him, tell him to come back over tomorrow night.

I say to bring close-toed shoes.

* * *

When he knocks on my door, the first thing I do is check his feet. He has sneakers on. Dark ones. I tell him they're perfect and make him follow me back down to the basement.

He asks me if I want to see his finger. After last night I stowed the nail back in its box, nestling it amongst the bed of sharp objects, then put myself to bed, giddy with the knowledge of what was going to happen tonight. I couldn't sleep at first, so I shoved out of bed and reopened the box. I took everything out and then reorganized the space, creating a perfect sized hole right where I imagine it will belong. I care about his fingernail, sure, but not as much as I care about what we're doing next.

He shows me his finger anyway.

I hold his hand in mine as I inspect the bare nail bed. The skin is scabbing. I lift it to my lips and give it a kiss, and then I press the pad of my thumb onto the excoriated flesh. He sucks in a breath but doesn't say anything.

He asks me what's next.

I tell him to take off his shoe and his sock.

Which one, he asks.

I don't give a shit.

He bends down to do what I say, and I kneel down to pull out the box. I need something larger than nail clippers this time. The sound of clanging metal rings out for a moment, and I pull out the cable cutters.

He takes off both shoes, but not his socks yet. I shuffle forward on my knees and rest a palm on the white fabric. It's a little damp from being in his sneakers all day. It should disgust me, but really, it just reminds me that he's alive under the cotton, and that soon even more of him will belong to me. I ask him if I can have the big toe. I honestly don't expect him to refuse me, but he does.

Okay fine, your pinky then.

He asks me, don't I need it for balance?

The reply is weird enough to draw my attention up from his feet.

Huh? I say.

He looks very seriously down at me, says, I heard somewhere that that's what your pinky toe is for. If you're missing your pinky, you can't keep your balance, and you'll just fall right over.

I roll my eyes. That's the stupidest shit I've ever heard, I say.

Oh.

Take off your sock.

He bends down to slip it off. His toes are clean, the nails are neat.

He suggests we get a towel.

God, he's so right. My boy is so smart.

I drag a pair of sweatpants out of the dirty laundry and fold them up neatly beneath his foot. I recommend he sits, actually, and he does.

I slip the bottom blade of the cutters beneath his little toe, nestle the digit right in the crook of the tool. He's staring at me with a vulnerability so intense that it makes my stomach cramp. I tell him how much I'm going to take care of it, how it already has a space of its own, how it'll be right next to the fingernail and the thatch of hair, how I can't wait to have more of him to keep.

Do you still trust me? I ask, so breathless I'm barely able to get the words out.

He nods once, very firm.

This is the best idea I've ever had, I say, and then I squeeze.

* * *

Turns out, his balance was mostly fine. We balled up a threadbare no-show sock and shoved it into his shoe to staunch the bleeding, but it bled less than I thought it would. Afterward, I cradled his hot, flushed head in my hands and told him how good he did, how happy he made me, how I was going to keep him safe in my box and no one was ever going to find him.

He told me he loved me.

It was the first time he ever said that, and my chest felt full and thick and my eyes prickled with wetness. I rolled his gift between my fingers, the most precious thing, and told him I loved him back.

When his mom knocked on the front door an hour later, she said he looked feverish and asked if he was getting sick and I told her sorry, my air conditioner isn't working. He nodded along.

I can't stop checking the box. I can't believe I'm so lucky. My gifts are lined up so nice and pretty, soft and supple amidst the sharp objects, the dangers threatening them at every opportunity. I kiss each of them and tuck the box under the covers with me to sleep.

I don't hear from my boy for almost a week, and so I message him first: come over. His reply comes quickly: my mom thinks we're having sex.

That makes me laugh. It shouldn't come as a surprise to me that what we have would be so misrepresented, so minimized and sanitized, that to the average person, sex is as deep and intimate an act as two people can share. They simply can't conceptualize anything close to what we have.

I type back the exact truth: no, what we're doing is better.

My boy tells me his mother planned a trip to visit his grandmother out of town. Anxiety floods me because there's no way he can leave me, especially not now. I say he needs to come up with something, and so he tells her that actually, yes, he is starting to feel sick after all, and hmm, it's probably a fever or something. Pretty bad idea to risk passing the flu to someone so elderly, he says. And it works. His mother and sister will be gone all week. So he packs a bag and comes over.

We lay together on the bed while something crackles on the small television in the corner. He's watching the show, but I'm too distracted to pay attention. My fingertips pet his naked one, no longer weepy and swollen and shiny. It's dulled down, the raw skin beginning to heal. The patch of hair on the back of his head has grown out some, no longer spiky when I run my hand through it. The parts he gave to me are regrowing. Returning to him. Cheapening the value of my gifts. The thought makes me sick.

There is one less bump in the sock of his right foot, however, and that's never going to change.

I wrap my arms tight around his middle and feel his breaths move his body. I'm afraid to ask for what I want, even though he's never denied me. My beautiful boy knows me better than anyone else, so he asks me.

What is it, he asks.

I want something bigger, I say.

You know I'll give you anything, he says.

It might be something you don't want to give.

He tells me he'll give me anything, so long as he can give it, and I make him promise before I pull out my box.

* * *

This time we didn't need something sharp. I realized that all we needed was a melon baller from the kitchen upstairs. The eye came out with very little resistance, but he panicked anyway. He screamed so loud that my eardrums hurt a little. I hoped it wouldn't cause any ringing. That would be so annoying.

I planned for the mess this time, so I had gauze and surgical tape tucked away in my box and was able to help him cover the wound. After, I cradled my gift in my oil slick palms. I didn't want to clean it off right away, it was just right, just the way it came. My boy apologized for yelling, but I told him he did amazing. I promised him I would take care of his gift forever and thank you, thank you for giving it to me.

He nodded, and maybe tried to say something else, but instead lay down and fell asleep.

Now, hours later, the basement bedroom is hot and humid and neither of us wants to leave. He's in some pain but doesn't complain very much. I tell him all the ways I'm going to look after my gift, how I'll hold it and tell it stories of my day and it'll feel like he's right there, watching me right back. I want so desperately to look under his bandage, but I know that's for another day. It's so dark. The television's off. We lie still, nothing but the sounds of our breath filling the space. I can tell he's still awake. I tell him he can't go home now, that he has to stay with me. The sheets are damp, and I can't tell if it's from the sweat or the blood, but I lean in close anyway. There's a coppery smell that hurts my teeth on the inhale. He asks me what he's supposed to do about his mom, but I don't answer. I scoop the prize I've been cradling and tuck it into my box. This one's even softer and more delicate amongst the metallic threats, and so I decide to wrap it in plastic for the time being.

He asks about his mom again, and this time I tell him to go to sleep.

* * *

The next couple days bleed together like watercolor. There's a stink in the room that we can't air out. The sheets need to be changed, and we need showers, but I'm too overwhelmed to leave the room. Everything I need is here. I have my sweet boy, and I have my box. I take trips to the kitchen to bring soft foods like yogurt and pudding, because now that he has no teeth, they're all he can eat.

I take pleasure in rattling them in my box like a maraca. I shimmy my shoulders and sing simple tunes to my boy, and he claps his hands because talking hurts and his gums are still swollen. He knows I'm disappointed that we couldn't get all twenty-eight out. Some of them in the back were stuck in his gums pretty hard. I make a joke about how jealous I am that the molars were taken out the previous year, and does that mean he's cheating on me with his dentist now? He makes a sound that sort of sounds like a laugh.

I peel off the rest of his fingernails like paint chips while we watch some reality show. I drop them in my box one by one while a panel votes on which contestant deserves elimination. The muted little pings of fingernails against metal make me happy, but the feeling is fleeting. It doesn't give me the same thrill it used to. Something's been aching inside me. Once again, I need more, and both of us know the question that's dancing on my tongue.

Do you love me? I ask him.

You know I do.

I tell him that I want something bigger this time. He doesn't reply at first. His one eye looks at me. He doesn't blink. His lips are swollen and chapped, and I wipe away a slight string of blood from his cheek.

Eventually, he says ok.

I say, I want something you may not be able to give me. I tell him I want something from inside him.

He doesn't immediately deny me. I tell him to say something.

It's cliche to want my heart, he slurs.

Okay, what then?

He doesn't respond.

What are you willing to give me? I ask.

His mouth tightens at the corners and he says, I ate something.

I'm not sure how to reply, so I don't.

I want you to have it, he tells me.

I understand his meaning. I light a cigarette, prop it between his lips, and my fingers tremble as I open my box. My paring knife is sharp and clean and I tell him it'll do the trick. I'm pretty sure I know where the stomach is, so I lean him back and he lifts his shirt. I'm surprised how much pressure I need to apply. I thought my blade was sharp, but it's dragging, and the resistance feels all wrong.

I don't stop.

The opening grows and it's not long until I can reach inside. My boy is saying something, or he's shouting something, but my pulse is so loud in my ears I can't make it out. My vision blurs at the periphery and the only thing I can see is how my hand disappears into his middle, and it's like a goddamn miracle what he's letting me do.

My fingers are slippery when I reach the stomach. Using my other hand, I bring the knife back down and cut through some more. I don't know how long I'm in there. It feels so quick, and then there it is.

My fingers brush against something hard and small. I pinch it and drag it out. It's round, some hard plastic material, about the size of a box of matches. The blood and viscera makes it hard to see. I lean in close and wipe the object as clean as I can, but the sun is setting and the room is obscured in shadow. My boy makes a sound, but I just can't look at him right now. My hands tremble as I wipe and wipe and wipe.

Finally, the shape makes sense to me, and the air leaves my lungs.

It's a jar of honey, I breathe.

My boy's mouth is smeared red. He smiles and it's a clown smile. He nods once, confirms, says it's from his little sister's kitchen playset.

I hold the toy, the honeypot, to my chest like it's our child. We gave meaning to something. My boy carried it for me, and I helped him birth it to life. I hold it close, like a father holding his newborn baby, proud of newfound parenthood, and proud of the blood, sweat, and mucus my partner gave to bring me this life, and I tell him it's beautiful, that he's beautiful. I tell him I love him.

I tell him, you're a beautiful thing.

Patti Smith
SLEAT
EY DIG ME
orship e old g

ALL HANDS ON THE BAD ONE

Kayli Scholz

Female Trouble's fans were mad at me. You could even say they were furious, threatening to pulverize my bones and drain my cerebrospinal fluid into the reservoir of a fog machine on the stage of a dingy venue called The Cretin. All because I'd harped on my assumption that the band members were demonic phantoms in inescapable rock-star disguises, and their songs were a little too good, if you know what I mean.

From the outside looking in, Female Trouble, (named after the 1974 John Waters film), is a punk band from Florida that overcame sexist adversity and successfully earned their big break in more forward-thinking places, like the Buc-ees parking lot opening in Texarkana.

I, Dawn Pudding, wore many hats. Some might even call me a poly band bandit. My troubles started when, all in one breath, I introduced myself to Female Trouble and hired myself to be their band manager, as we talked on the sidewalk of some asshole Republican governor's campaign rally protest. I wasn't below hoodwinking these women into believing that I was an undercover investigative reporter, although I'd never written anything or had any noteworthy life experiences outside of riding the rails at rock shows across the eastern seaboard. I wanted to expose Female Trouble for their backstage ritual obscenities and ostensibly *foul* recording sessions.

Female Trouble's reputation wasn't like Ozzy biting the head off a bat, or a G.G. Allin wardrobe malfunction. It wasn't L7's Donita Sparks pulling a bloody tampon out of her vag midsong and pitching it into the front row. It wasn't Dave Matthews Band dumping eight-hundred pounds of waste from their bus's shitter tank into the Chicago River. And it most definitely wasn't Taylor Swift diving through an AI-generated on-stage ocean as pristine as a Windows 95 screensaver. No, Female Trouble was worse, possibly satanic, and toxic– some real sickos. They turned their audiences nuclear, horny, screwball, hungry for a snack–literally, as all that adrenaline made one famished, seizing into song and dance like an exfoliating clown on bath salts.

Whatever was happening here, I'd get to the bottom of it.

At the campaign rally protest, Female Trouble played their song "Get a Grip" to a bystander Republican committee that got so flummoxed at these angry women singing that their wet farts faded the stars and stripes on the backdropped American flag. There was even a battered, bleeding manikin head on a stick, fashioned to look as much as possible like the Governor himself, with dildos sticking out of every nostril, ear-hole, and, was either a mouth or an asshole– it was hard to tell these days. Fans were invited up on stage to fuck the manikin skull during the song. Naturally, these sorts of crowd participation shindigs were unacceptable in the Buc-ees parking lot itself, because daytime shoppers wouldn't have appreciated having to wait in double lines for their beaver nuggets and banana pudding. So the sidewalk protest would have to suffice.

Female Trouble is Darcy, the lead singer, Scuz, the guitarist, Sloane, the drummer, and Finn, the bassist. (Finn's fans called themselves 'finnies').

Following my appointment as their manager, Female Trouble invited me to an invite-only special show where one of their biggest fans was on the verge of death. They were asked not to tote the manikin skull to the show, because the young woman's grandmother was sensitive to death and constantly worried about The Purge. I agreed to haul their instruments up fourteen flights of stairs, eager to show them my prowess and athleticism, not needing to take the elevator or disassemble the drum kit.

Well, that's when it all came to a heed.

There, on the fourteenth-floor dwelling, was a young woman sinking into a filthy hole in her couch, covered in pressure ulcers, with maggot larvae in the corners of her eyes; the ideal place for colonization, given how much fangirl crying she'd done over Female Trouble's song "Couch Potato". Her caretaker, a granny who also loved the band, informed us that "Couch Potato" inspired her granddaughter's alternative lifestyle and, yes, she'd succumb to her internal injuries eventually, but in the meantime, it was her dream to meet Darcy, Scuz, Sloane, and Finn.

Because there was nowhere to sit down, what with the granddaughter sinking into the crusty couch, I watched from the kitchen pantry as the band ripped into their set. They played "Get a Grip," "2044 Peak Boomer Death," and the song that brought them here, "Couch Potato." I swiped a squirming maggot off my ear, swatted at a fruit fly, and clapped politely after each song, with the granny fist pumping through each verse. I could tell she'd opened a mosh pit once or twice, back in her day. I observed how crudely the band arranged themselves around their instruments, like in the shape of a medieval satanic rhombus. I wondered what the granny knew about medieval satanic rhombus' as her granddaughter took her final breath and the couch cushions settled like an old house, engulfing her in a ring of black smoke. Despite Couch Potato's death, Female Trouble signed autographs and took selfies with the granny. (And, right hand to God, I saw Scuz sign her name with the denomination 6-6-6.)

The next day was show day. I donned a tweed detective hat and held a giant magnifying glass at arm's length, watching fans corral outside the dingy Cretin venue by the stage door. The graffitied square building was surrounded by dense forest and all the Florida scrubland you could endure out here in the middle of nowhere. Some of these women had been in line for years, *ages*, waiting for a band like Female Trouble to come and save them from some soul-crushing, listless life-turned-Armageddon. And, as the band's manager, private detective, and roadie, I observed the spectacular attitudes of how the Good Ones waited in line versus how the Bad Ones waited in line.

The Good Ones waited patiently, not *too* enthused, because that would have been embarrassing. Too much giddiness could make you look like a stalker, or a potential psycho killer. The Good Ones committed to buying the records, not just streaming them, buying the B-sides, and giving up their sons and pig-tail-haired daughters for a potential setlist. The Bad Ones pushed and shoved, only acknowledging the band's earliest analog recordings, and refusing to listen to anything marginally evolved in their repertoire. The Bad Ones were the gatekeepers of punk rock and still pretended to care about all-male bands. (All-male bands were still, for some reason, a thing.) And most of all, they refused to admit that something fishy was percolating behind the scenes.

I approached a woman named Misty, nicknamed 'Mist,' whose eyes had surely seen the devil in Female Trouble's music. Her eyes lacked sleep and vitamin A.

"Hey, what's their secret?" I said. "You can tell me. I'm an insider."

"Female Trouble?" Mist lifted a pierced eyebrow, indulging me. She offered me a stick of Fruit Stripe gum, but I refused. I was trying to cut back. "Their secret's not out yet. But it will be. Once we hear the song."

"What song?"

"The new song. The one that's gonna change everything."

"Change it - how?"

"You a cop?"

"Fuck no," I said.

Mist laughed and, although I wasn't sure if she was laughing with me or at me, I took it as a sign of trust. "Get in line with the rest of us and maybe you'll find out."

"Guess we're in our fuck around and find out era," I said.

Mist didn't crack a smile.

"Well, what can you tell me about the secret song?"

"They haven't played it live yet. But when they do—get ready. Rumor has it you can only hear it on a special pair of headphones. So, you dig a hole in the woods for the headphones to work. So, you sit in a hole, kind of like your grave, and put the headphones on." She popped another Zebra Stripe gum. "It changes you, charges you like a battery. You're connected to it on a cellular level."

I wrote that down: 'cellular level.'

"Some fans think Scuz is a real hardass because she came up with the digging your grave thing, but she's a real softie at heart. I even watched her eat an ice cream once."

I wrote that down, too: 'ice cream.'

Out of nowhere, I sensed an evil permeating from the stage door. It was time for me to meet the band in the woods in an uncharted, dangerous cave with a sign out front that read: **NO ENTRANCE UNLESS TAKING PHOTOS FOR ALBUM COVER.**

"That's us," said Darcy, and the five of us hiked into the pitch-black darkness, sidestepping skulls and bones and sharp daggers sticking out of still-beating hearts and a pancreas.

We came upon what I assumed was a cryptic ancient warning. The type that could only be deciphered by somebody that had studied demonology. But as I led the way with the band's guitars strapped to my ass, I realized that my cryptic, ancient-warnings-on-the-cave walls were just English cursive.

"Not to worry," I said to myself sheepishly.

The show was that night, and I only had a matter of hours to get the band to admit to their morally corrupt crimes; to expose this madness before their audience turned phantom, too. Finn, by some miraculous phenomenon, built a campfire and we sat round robin fashion, drinking Capri-Suns while looking pensively into the flames. I had to keep pretending to be their friend, medic, therapist, and pastor, not just their band manager and investigative reporter/detective. I asked them about their day jobs. Surely playing a Buc-ees parking lot and The Cretin wasn't enough to pay the bills. Not in this economy.

"Not in this economy," I said, to sound like I knew a lot about economics and how bad things were getting.

But just as I suspected, Sloane wouldn't admit she was a Ouija board builder and gravedigger by day. Scuz was also looking a little … pale. Ghost-like. And Darcy's singing could surely be traced back to haunting fans through their crud-crusted earbuds and stereo speakers. Finn, too. Who in their right mind chooses to play bass? Was the band a vessel for the living dead? How long had they been dead for? I thought the zombies vs. rockers thing ended in 2022, but maybe I was wrong.

Maybe Dave Grohl had really been onto something.

The band suggested I take layout pictures for their new album, *Rush Hour Renegades*. Scuz suggested something bold, so I had the four of them squeeze through a dark crawlspace where oxygen was scarce, and a foreboding green ray of light emitted from a creaking tomb buried in the walls. The black-and-white filter on my phone made the pictures appear almost professional. After the photos, we sat around the campfire some more.

"You gals ever write any songs out here?" I asked.

"We don't write the songs," Scuz said. "The songs write us."

"Well," I said, eager to share. I picked up a stick from the fringes of the fire and put it in my mouth like I'd seen Clint Eastwood do in a movie trailer once. "That's not what I heard from one of your fans at The Cretin. Someone says you have a special pair of headphones that only work if you're six feet underground."

Their conspiratorial glances told me everything I needed to know, and just as I was about to duck and run before they could decapitate me and feed me to the fire, Sloane leaned forward. Our shadows crawled across the cave walls as the fire crackled between us. A wolf howled in the distance and a bat with the striking visage of Vincent Price flew over our heads.

Sloane said, "How would you like to, *you know?*"

I leaned into the fire, too, our sweating noses almost touching like pig snouts in a pen. "Ask me," I said.

"Dig your own grave to wear the headphones?"

The rest of the band leaned forward, too, and then, before we all caught on fire, I agreed to dig my own grave under the gross sun, to climb down, and to listen to the secret song on the secret headphones.

It's a lot of work digging your own grave.

I didn't want to be *that person* and mention how they'd probably make bank at their merch table selling future burial plots with stop-motion band cut-outs like the Halloween decorations at Home Depot. Instead, I just plunged that shovel so hard and so fast into the earth, digging until callouses the size of Couch Potato's pressure ulcers punctured my skeleton, and, for a hot minute, I was nothing but bones in a tweed detective cap. A rock journalist's job is never easy, and it comes at a price.

It was time.

I skidded, feet-first into the sunken, damp, skunky earth as worms vined into fallen chickweed, and between the gaps of my teeth. Besides the crows eating the dead out of their respectable graves, and the occasional power chord being played in the distance, it was silent.

"I'm ready," I said.

Sloane and Darcy stood to the left of my grave, Scuz and Finn to the right. Scuz bent down and placed the big puffy headphones firmly over my head.

And the song played.

I don't know what happened after that because I blacked out.

I awoke in the motel room, alone, confused, and with the anxiety that I'd once diagnosed myself with after doom scrolling on a grief subReddit about grieving for '90s nostalgia, flaring up. (Some people were really suffering out there.) I sat up in bed and tried remembering what the rhythm of the song was like, how the lyrics went, anything at all.

Nothing.

My suspicions about Female Trouble were confirmed: Female Trouble was a satanic, drugged-out, devil-worship band that was so morally corrupt they've got fans voluntarily digging their own graves for their own wisecracking, sick amusement. There was no secret song, and those headphones were just from the latest Fisher Price line-up, or whatever they were calling waves of gadgets these days.

I paced the motel room, thinking about my personal Watergate as I watched creepy Old Man Winters sweeping leaves in crop circle patterns. I shook my head, dumbfounded. What had our mothers taught us? And what was it good for? Don't wear a ponytail because somebody like Old Man Winters will grab you by that ponytail and lure you into a van filled with your favorite candy. And don't attend a party and hydrate because a predator will drop some toxic sludge into your drink, and you'll collapse and die, pregnant and alone. Don't go to rock shows by yourself. You were asking for it.

This wouldn't be the first time I'd stood up for my fellow man and what really mattered. I'd defended emo and pop-punk to the ends of the earth. You couldn't have hardcore without emo, dumbass! There was a fucking fundamental difference between west coast and east coast rap. Country western was just a nametag invented to keep "hillbillies" from enjoying the fruits of their labor, and I'd stood at the stage doors like our forefathers once had, educating people that queercore and grunge and riot grrrl were not the same thing, but nice try! If you can't differentiate new-wave and post-punk and shoegaze, you don't deserve to be here! You couldn't have chicken without the egg!

I had to warn Female Trouble's fans.

I had to be the millennial we wanted to see in the world.

At the venue, I knew that keeping cool, calm, and collected was key to not drawing attention to myself. I passed Mist at the bar, approached a security guard, and flashed a backstage pass. Sure, it was actually a Costco shopping card with my picture in the corner, but who could tell?

Backstage was unremarkable.

I rummaged through Darcy's bag, taking evidence of ibuprofen powder on a silver spoon. I picked through Finn's wallet, removed a suspicious credit card with the word 'Discover' on it — what did she have to discover? The devil? — I played four rounds of spider solitaire, cross referenced Scuz's dental records with Sloane's childhood immunization records, making sure things were up to code. I inspected a hairbrush with some cagey blue hairs that reminded me of the Smurf Christmas special, napped, built a birdhouse, learned to crochet, and finally, wrote in black marker on their set list: **DAWN PUDDING TAKES A STAND AGAINST THE BAND**, followed by three exclamation marks.

"You wanna play hardball?" I asked out loud. "Let's play hardball."

It was almost showtime.

I pushed my way to the front of the crowd as the lights came down and the seductive white noise got replaced by booming cheers. Female Trouble walked out one by one like it was *no big deal*. Couch Potato's granny crowd surfed over women half her age in the front row, her walking cane gliding against the rail and bonking everybody over the head. Collectively, the body odor was as bottomless and stinky as a bloomin' onion at the Outback, but I wasn't going anywhere. Women cried, screamed, vomited into each other's mouths. A fire broke out after Nerf bullets ripped through the roof, spraying everybody with confetti and foam. One young woman, covered in buttons, ate soup and crackers. A stampede of zebras and tigers from the local zoo showed up wearing band merch.

The crowd had become like ants in the pants, but worse. I thought about videoing it for evidence-sake but thought better of it, as several fans in the crowd donned shirts stitched with the words: **STOP VIDEOING CONCERTS**. Meanwhile, another fan had proved their worthiness by cutting out her heart and hooking it up to the monitor mix so it would beat in rhythm to "Get a Grip". (The heart can, in fact, still beat outside of the body. It's a scientific fact.) And lastly, I'd heard through the grapevine of Female Trouble's fans *edging* their concert experience to make the night last as long as possible, a new phenomenon in the southern punk scene, one that the band had acknowledged, but couldn't participate in. (Eventually, the band would put their jim-jams on for bedtime one leg at a time, just like everybody else.)

After they played "Get a Grip," it was time.

I mustered my courage, became sturdy as a tree in the storm, then I jumped over the rail, mauled four young women, and climbed the stage as the band scratched their heads at **DAWN PUDDING TAKES A STAND AGAINST THE BAND!!!(?)**

The crowd looked at me with scorn. I grabbed Darcy's mic stand and dragged it in front of me, the feedback prickling the room as everybody's hair blew sideways. The band, hopped up on ibuprofen and acetaminophen, exchanged baffled glances. Security seemed to know that whatever this was going to be, it was important.

"My name is Dawn Pudding."

The crowd booed, throwing a sweat rag at me and a tomato.

But I kept going.

"I'm Female Trouble's band manager. I'm also their friend, confidant, nurse, pastor, bookkeeper, housekeeper, creative consultant, therapist, photographer, journalist, cousin fourth removed, and roadie. I'm also a private detective and this is my inaugural investigation."

The crowd's adrenaline had exhausted, and the fires were extinguished. The young woman who was eating soup and crackers quit doing so.

I raised my fist, gripping the mic. "This band, they're not who they say they are! They're not real! They're the living-dead, evil phantoms that conjure demons in a cave! Play their songs backwards, and you'll go mad! But you won't even know you're going mad because you'll black out in a mysterious grave! They don't run on music, they run on trouble! It's a cult! It's depravity! They're fakes! I can prove it!"

The crowd gasped.

"Wait a second," Darcy said, taking the mic back. "We're not the living-dead and we don't participate in demonic rituals."

Scuz took the mic from Darcy. She faced the restless and weirded out crowd. "Yeah," said Scuz. "We've always been about the music and bringing people together."

I grabbed the mic from Scuz, "then how come you've got fans digging in cemeteries in the blistering heat just to hear some unreleased satanic song?"

Scuz gently lifted the mic. "It wasn't a cemetery; it was the woods. And it wasn't satanic, it was entrapment."

I didn't bother taking the mic this time, but leaned over it so everybody could hear me. "Entrapment?"

Darcy snagged the mic from Scuz. "Yes. We thought you were going to hear the song and upload it to some YouTube channel or Napster."

"Napster hasn't been around for, like, twenty-five years," I said.

"The point is," Darcy continued. "We thought you might be one of the bad ones. But the truth is, we were wrong, and you stuck up not only for yourself, but for our fans. You care. That's why you dug your grave, Dawn."

I took the mic back. "But … if you're not practicing satanic ritual, how did Finn make a campfire out of thin air?"

Sloane took the mic this time. "People have been making campfires for warmth and light since the beginning of man."

"Oh," I said. "Gee, I hadn't thought of it that way."

I realized, standing there in front of the flabbergasted crowd, what being a band manager and detective was all about. It was recognizing the truth and giving it the freedom to let go. I encouraged Female Trouble to sing their new song and, whatever pandemonium broke out, so be it.

And pandemonium it was.

Because this three-chord song was played just enough out of tune, it resurrected an ancient deity whose name, in Latin, translated to 'Half a Brain,' who wiped out all the bottom feeders in the U.S. of A. This included, but was not limited to, lawmakers that had ever denied a transgender person's bodily autonomy, Nazi's, racists, bigots, misogynists, pedophiles, corporate numbskulls, bad poets, billionaires, and anybody that had ever dressed up as Uncle Sam for Halloween. If a bottom feeder heard the song, in earbuds or headphones or bluetooth-this or bluetooth-that, it sent them into a stir-crazy convulsion. They ripped their large intestines out and devoured their teeth and hair until they choked from the terror, so awful to watch, but you couldn't look away.

"We did it!" I exclaimed, hours after a chunk of the world's population had incinerated themselves and, essentially, been swallowed up by a three-chord song.

And as I danced and sang alongside Female Trouble's fans, our grabby, sweaty, grungy hands reaching into the air, I thought, "This is how the musicians on the Titanic must've felt as they played together as the ship sank into the Atlantic and thousands of people drowned in zero-below temperatures." Man, and that guitar. Scuz played like it was an extra limb; it was a guitar you'd want to spend the night and watch Netflix with, quietly. The world was a better place without numbskulls. I used to think the most dangerous, adrenaline-fueled missions involved traipsing through Kuwait or Jacksonville, Florida, but, no, it was all about singing at the rock show with your friends and some focused musicians. A spectacle. Talk about girls to the front.

IAN A. BAIN

UNTIL EVERY CAGE IS EMPTY // UPROAR

Ian A. Bain

My entire world was a concrete room.

There were no windows, no birds, no buzzing insects.

There was only ever the buzzing of the bright fluorescent lights.

I'd spent all of my life—what I remembered of it—strapped to a table, set on an incline.

I wasn't completely alone.

The man in the white lab coat walked across the room to a metal table, cluttered with scalpels, drills, and forceps. His bald head shined and his beady eyes leered like hungry black voids. A tattoo of a long surgical knife ran from the man's elbow to his wrist. I did not know the man's name, but I knew he was in charge. There were others in white lab coats, all taking their torturing orders from the bald man.

They used me to test their new tools, their surgical techniques, and their tonics. Sometimes they dusted me with powders. Sometimes the powders didn't hurt. Sometimes they only tingled or itched. And sometimes they burned. One time they put dust on my arm and it felt as though they'd taken a torch to my skin. I screamed, and the people in white lab coats just watched and diligently took notes on their clipboards. My skin blistered, bubbled, and slipped off my arm. I couldn't see it, but I could hear my liquified flesh plop on the cold floor. Either as a kindness, or perhaps just to stop the annoyance of my screams, they plunged a needle into my arm.

When I woke up, the arm they'd dusted was different. Before, it had been hairless, smooth, black. But after I woke up, my arm was covered in fur, and long, black claws stuck out where, before, there had been human fingernails.

Any time the white coats inflicted irreparable damage to my limbs, I would awake the next day with replacements. One day I might have long, elegant, bone-white legs, and the next day I would wake up with stubby, hairy legs. I didn't know where this endless supply of limbs came from, but I also didn't ponder it that frequently. I knew so little of the outside world then, I assumed it must have been normal.

It wasn't always dust they put on my skin.

Sometimes they put fabric on my body and blew fire at me. Other times they forced liquids into me through tubes and needles. I got submerged in a large tank of water until I lost consciousness. Sometimes they shot liquids in my bloodstream and told me it would stop me from feeling pain. To test this, they removed my foot with a saw. The concoction in my blood didn't work, and I felt every tooth on the blade as it bit into my flesh, over and over again, until it crunched through bone.

Another time they gave me a shot and told me the compound would, "enhance my experience of life, help me feel everything in life more: feel more love, more arousal, more excitement, just…*more*." To test this drug, they once again sawed off a foot. The chemicals worked that time; I felt every tooth even more than before.

No matter what product the white coats used on me, whether it was a vial of liquid, a canister of powder, or a flamethrower, they all bore the same green label.

I don't know why they tortured me, or why they needed a living person to test their tortures on. They did not seem to particularly delight in my torture, but they also did not seem guilty about it. They too, it seemed, had become mentally numb.

***

The white coats were not the only visitors I had in that concrete room. There was a boy who visited me from time to time. The top of the boy's head was missing. He always stood in the farthest, darkest corner of the room, and mostly visited after the white coats were gone. His yellow eyes would peer at me, and I'd be afraid to sleep. But he'd keep staring at me, never saying a word, until exhaustion made me fall asleep despite myself. Whenever the boy bent forward, I saw the open cavity of his head. Where brains should have been, I saw nothing but a puddle of blood.

The boy seemed to delight in my revulsion; he'd grin whenever I squirmed. Most of the time though, he just watched. But the boy didn't watch me like the white coats did. The white coats stared at me expectantly, carefully. Instead, the boy stared at me vacantly, like he wasn't all there. It was more like he was the remnant of a boy, instead of an actual, whole boy. There was something missing besides the top of his head.

Occasionally, the boy would appear when the white coats were there. I don't think they could see him, or else maybe young boys with missing skull caps were a normal occurrence in their line of work.

Eventually, others came too, always standing in the back corner, near the boy.

There was the large woman with only one leg. Where a second leg should have jutted from her hip, she dripped viscera. Every time I saw her, time after time, there was always blood dripping from the wound. I wondered how she never ran out. Her arms and fingers were gnarled at chaotic angles, like the cracks in the concrete of my room. One arm was completely backwards, as if the arm was detachable and the last person to twist it back in went one turn too many. Her neck was bent so that she must've seen the world sideways. Up was right and right was down. One eye bulged too far out of her head and looked like it was filled with too much blood. But this woman never remarked at her physical condition, not that I ever heard. And so, I wondered: If she was real, how long had she been like this to have gotten used to it?

Some of these apparitions weren't human.

There was a massive silver gorilla. There were monkeys, pigs and cows.

Even a tiger. But, just like the humans who appeared in the room, each of the animals that appeared were missing something. Hands, legs, heads, sometimes skin.

For the longest time, I wondered what these voyeurs wanted, and if I should fear them more than the white coats.

***

One day I awoke to find one of the white coats standing on a ladder in the room. This was not the man in the white coat, but instead, he was one of his underlings. He was turning the black box in the corner away from me, towards the concrete wall. Then he stepped down off the ladder and came to me. I was taken aback at first, because this man had emotion on his face. He was not mentally numb like the rest of them. Was it worry on his face? Sadness?

He asked, "How are you?"

I tried to speak, but all that came out was a gurgling sound.

"I thought many times of leaving, quitting, but I couldn't leave you… Even with your face the way it is now…I still see the young boy who was wheeled in here…"

The boy who was missing part of his head appeared, skulking in the far corner like he always did.

But, as usual, if the white coat noticed him, he didn't react. Instead, he just looked at me and said, "You are not a monster," and then the man loosened the straps that held me to the inclined table. I felt a sharp pinch and the man showed me a black oval-shaped thing he'd removed from the back of my neck. It blinked red and was a little smaller than the bugs I'd repeatedly seen scurrying around the room. The white coat dropped the oval to the floor and stomped on it twice. The red blinking stopped. Then he stepped back and pulled a needle from his coat. It looked just like the needles that they usually stabbed me with, complete with its neon green label. The man stuck the needle in his own neck and plunged. He smiled at me, then, seconds later, he was writhing on the floor.

I struggled off the table and lumbered forward with a limp. I could not remember walking, and my legs weren't the same length. It took me a few steps to figure out what I was doing, but each step became more coordinated than the last. I went around the man, still convulsing on the cold concrete floor, and was almost to the door when the room began to fill with smoke. It burned my skin, and when I breathed, it burned inside me. The man on the floor's skin sizzled and evaporated. The boy in the corner just watched with his usual vacant eyes.

It was not long before I joined the white coated man on the floor.

***

I awoke back on the table.

I lifted my head, bending my neck just enough to see that my flesh had transformed again: my legs white and hairy, but matching now. My torso was hairless and curvy. One arm looked like that of an animal, while the other was too short; a child's, perhaps.

The man in the white coat, the leader of all the white coats, saw that I was awake. He came to me and said softly, "You will never leave this place." Then the man turned and played with some machinery on a black metal cart.

Through my new skin, all I felt was cold, metal, and defeat. Whatever the reason, whatever crime I committed before I was on the table–for I always thought I did have some sort of a life before the concrete room that I just couldn't remember–I truly believed I was never going to leave that place.

As my mind was resigning to what the rest of existence would be, pairs of yellow eyes appeared around me. I hadn't noticed the remnants of people and animals approaching me, but all at once, they stood around my table, leering. The man in the white coat spoke to his helpers and they wheeled the black cart around to my side. My eyes met one of the helpers', and I saw how much he feared me, and I wondered why. Was I so monstrous, so terrifying? Was that why they had chosen me to live on the table?

They attached pads on wires to my skin. Sweat beads formed on their faces.

The leader of the white coats approached me, and his assistants walked away. He placed his fingers on a dial in the middle of the black machine to which I was connected, and for the first time, I saw him smile.

The lights overhead flickered each time they electrocuted me. I flinched and shut my eyes. They shocked me three times, but before they could shock me a fourth, they were interrupted by a scream.

When I opened my eyes, the machine's pads were no longer attached to me.

Instead, they were all over the assistant's face.

The assistant looked around, confused, eyebrows slanted down and eyes bulging in terror.

The remnants had surrounded him, but still, I didn't know if he saw them.

The boy who was missing half of his head grasped the machine's dial and cranked it as far as it would turn, until the assistant shook violently and smoke rose from his skin. When the boy turned off the machine, the assistant fell to the floor, twitched once more, then lay still.

The other white coats began to panic, looking in all directions for whatever had fried their friend. They could not see the others, the remnants, in the room.

The one-armed gorilla picked up a man, and while he held him, suspended in midair, a monkey pulled wiring from the ceiling and wrapped it many times around the man's neck.

The gorilla hauled the man downward, violently, like it was trying to slam the man against the ground.

The white coat's neck didn't break. He didn't die instantly. Instead, he swung, struggling, until he stopped breathing.

The tiger pounced on an assistant's back and pinned her to the floor. It dug its teeth into her back and ripped a part of her spine out as an old man in a hospital gown picked up scalpels from the metal table and, faster than any real human could have moved, he plunged every instrument of torture into the eyes and ears of another assistant.

The leader ran for the door and hammered on the heavy steel to be let out. But nobody let him out.

Perhaps the others had already run away, afraid to release whatever was inside the room. Or maybe they wanted the remnants to finish off the white coats. Maybe they wanted to leave no witnesses. Maybe they didn't like the white coats, just like the white coats didn't like me. Whatever the reason, those who were outside the concrete room did not open the door and did not save the white coats from slaughter.

The last assistant alive joined the leader in banging on the steel door as the large woman with the missing leg hopped towards the assistant and forced herself inside him through his back. The assistant ripped off his shirt and tried grasping at whatever he felt on his back. The one-legged woman did not need to open his skin to move inside him, but I saw as his skin bubbled and stretched and his muscles shifted around. The assistant's ribs expanded and broke away from his spine, each bone on the verge of piercing his skin like they were hungry for the open air. He cried and fell to his knees. His arms bulged, his legs—or rather, *leg*– inflated, as did his stomach. He ballooned, bigger and bigger, until he popped. His flesh and blood and viscera covered the walls and his boss.

The man in the white coat stopped pounding on the door and began whimpering. What was left of his last assistant dripped down on him from the ceiling. He turned and slid down the door, until he was sitting with his knees pulled against his chest.

The remnants surrounded him.

The old man who had turned an assistant's face into a scalpel holder placed a box in front of the man in the white coat. The old man squatted, opened the box, and pulled a needle and a vial out.

Both were stickered with the neon green label.

The old man passed the needle to the woman with one leg, then gave a canister of white powder to one of the monkeys, who began to untwist the lid curiously. The old man continued to pass out the contents of the box until every remnant with opposable thumbs had something.

And then, one at a time, they began administering the man's treatment.

The monkey threw white powder in the man's face, and he screamed as his skin shriveled and fell off in globs. The leader slumped to his right, as if he was going to pass out, but the woman with one leg stuck a needle in his neck to wake him up again. More needles were stuck in him, liquids doused on him, pills were forced down his throat, and even for all the horrors the man had inflicted upon me, I could not keep watching.

The remnant of the young boy walked towards me, and at first I thought he was coming to set me free. But the boy smiled and grabbed my right leg where it met my hip. He wormed his little remnant fingers past the staples that held the leg to my hip until his hands disappeared into my flesh.

And then he began to pull.

I screamed in pain and confusion. The other remnants, apparently no longer consumed with the man in the white coat, joined the boy and dug their hands into the border of my leg and hip. It felt like they were trying to separate my body. They kept pulling until I heard a tear, a pop, and a crack. The remnants tossed my leg aside, then began to repeat the process with my other limbs.

Thankfully, I passed out.

***

When I awoke for the last time in the concrete room, I was alone. I sat up on the operating table, which had been set parallel with the floor while I was unconscious. The incline was gone. I rubbed my head as it throbbed violently. The floor was covered in bodies, and *parts* of bodies, and unrecognizable bits that used to be inside bodies.

I didn't see the man in the white coat anywhere.

The door to the room was open, and there were no sounds besides the pounding in my head and the buzz of fluorescent lights. I got off the table and fell to my knees.

New legs, again, but for the first time, clothed legs. Legs that looked identical in every way.

I managed to stand, using the table for support. Something on my arm caught my eye: a long tattoo of a scalpel.

I limped towards the door and paused.

Though the room had been my own hell, it was all I knew. My entire remembered existence had been within those four walls. I knew every crack, every spot of discoloration on the walls. I had not had a happy life there, but I couldn't help wondering, *What if the world outside is worse?*

But I had to find out.

On the other side of the door was a long hallway. On the right-hand side were windows which exposed laboratory equipment, also covered in blood and chunks of human.

I jumped when I saw a figure among the equipment.

The man in the white coat.

I put my hands up in defense, and he did the same.

I walked closer.

He did the same.

It was the man in the white coat, but it was also my reflection. In the window, I could just make out the haggard stitching along the top of my skull, the new skin stapled over the places where the remnants had applied the corrosive powders.

I smiled, perhaps for the first time, and continued on.

***

I found a clearing in a forest and collapsed by a log. The light was dim, and slowly getting dimmer. The buzzing and chirping and singing of the forest creatures wrapped me in a sonic blanket and made me feel weightless. I couldn't wait to discover what beings made those wonderful sounds.

At some point I'd drifted off, and when I came to, the world was dark but for a ray of moonlight that spilled through a hole in the tree canopy. I considered standing and exploring the forest, but felt when it was light again—whenever that might be—would be a better time for exploring. I noticed a set of yellow eyes among the trees.

I stood, and the being approached me.

I prayed that I was just seeing things, but standing before me was the man in the white coat.

This was not my reflection.

He had burn marks all over his skin, and his neck, where the remnants had stabbed him with needles, blisters the size of fists threatened to explode. His limbs were severed, but hung suspended in the air just where they would normally have dangled if they were attached.

He leered and grinned hungrily.

Now I see him every night.

Every morning.

I see him just as much as I saw him in the concrete room.

He follows me everywhere I go.

I've been waking up with burns and lacerations, just like I did in the room when they tested their powders and liquids and drugs on me.

The leader has not started torturing me when I'm awake, but I'm sure it's coming soon.

I just hope that the next time he removes my brain, he leaves it to rot.

I do not want him to find me a new host.

I do not want to become a remnant like the others.

I have seen the outside world. The forests and rivers and villages have replaced my four concrete walls. The sun and the moon have taken over from the noisy lights. I have heard the buzzing of insects, the singing of birds. I have seen the wonders of the world, and I am no longer afraid to die.

*Please note that any shifts in tense or style within this work are intentional and a reflection of the author's artistic choices. These changes are not errors and have been carefully considered by both the author and editor to enhance the narrative experience.

I WANNA BE YOUR DOG

J.R. Billingsley

Ronnie knows it isn't right that he needs her at that moment, in his room, with the rain beating down, lightning and thunder punctuating the roving storm with his bandmates lounging just beyond the door.

He wants her face to face, noses touching, her hand caressing him.

He wants to curl up beside her, but not as her equal. No. He wants to curl up at the foot of her bed. She could run her fingers down his spine or spank him for pissing on the carpet if she wanted to. If she was even willing to let him urinate. Or defecate. She could rub his nose in it. Smack his bottom and order him outside or back in the crate.

He particularly enjoyed the crate.

Ronnie closes his eyes, and he sees her. She's shifted again into that animal, but he knows that he is the pet. He sees her dilapidated ranch-style home in the blue collar neighborhood, the cage the only thing in her back bedroom where she'd replaced the carpet with newspaper. He desperately works to trigger his other senses. He longs to smell the cold stew she dumped nightly into his bowl, or the smell of the lit candles scattered around her home.

He listens past the rain falling outside and his bandmates tuning up in the other room, and he hopes to hear her scratchy, gravelly voice commanding him. "Sit, Ronnie." "Stay, Ronnie." "Fetch, Ronnie." "Kiss, Ronnie." "Suck, Ronnie." "Bad Ronnie." "Good Ronnie."

She had said little else while he was with her, but these phrases claw like the feedback and distortion from his amp. Even when Ronnie closes his mind to all other things, his other senses fail him. With every day that has passed since the rescue, memories of his time with her have faded a bit more. He wants to feel her hand again, fingers drumming or kneading his scalp, caressing his side, his shoulder, his arm, his thigh.

He shudders at the thought of her nails tickling his flesh in the tenderest of areas.

"What are you?" he asks aloud.

"What are you doing, man?" Ossie stands in the doorway to Ronnie's bedroom. Ronnie wonders when it was opened. Outside, a crack of lightning reveals her face in the deepest shadows of Ronnie's room, and the thunder, like a paradiddle on TomTom's snare, reminds him of her voice. Soon, the thunder will be close enough to thump like a bass.

"You okay?" Ossie doesn't care about a lot, but he cares about Ronnie.

Ronnie nods. "Just, remembering."

"If you wanna quit for tonight…" He steps into the room.

"No," Ronnie says, shaking his head.

"Shit," Ossie clenches a fist and shakes his head. "I knew it was too soon. You ain't ready, man, I'm sorry—"

"No," Ronnie says, cutting him off. "I'm fine. Just, remembering her."

Ossie claps his back. "Best you don't. Come on. We're ready to start."

* * *

They play. Ronnie knows it's loud, but his neighbors never complained before. Now, the old bat of a manager did. Called the cops on them. Threatened to evict him on several occasions. But she isn't usually around on Tuesday nights which was why he'd moved the practice.

They play grunge and ballads; Ronnie stretches from power chords to finger picking the rhythm, 12 bar blues and back. His mind swims in the smoke and stench of beer and Ossie sings and they shiver from what slinks in the shadows as Ronnie slips slowly into some trippy Pink Floyd rift. The apartment folds and rolls like the ocean and the smell of smoke is thick. Someone fills his glass. It doesn't matter who, or with what.

When Ronnie awakes for real, sober and not numb, a fact emphatically highlighted from his throbbing headache, all he knows is that it's sunny and the shadows are long, so that means its late in the day. He sits up in his bed and gets his bearings. His door is open and, in the living room, he hears shifting weight triggering the springs of his couch cushions. He staggers off his mattress and braces himself against the frame of his bedroom door as his eyes adjust to consciousness.

The girl wears slick black fur and squats over TomTom's torso, splayed out on the sofa. Ronnie only knows it's TomTom because he recognizes bits of the Grateful Dead tank top which the drummer always wears – but the torso has no head.

She smiles, a serpentine tongue flicking out from between her lips and tasting the air. Her right claw lifts a dollop of blood to her lips, and she purrs out a yummy sound.

She came back for him, after all.

His mind shuts off and the blackness is silent and refreshing. He loves the silence as much as he loves the noises *they* produce. He remembers the nights in her cage, and on her mattress, and how silent they were, and he loves this also, though he'll never admit it.

* * *

"You okay?"

Ossie again. Ronnie meets his friend's gaze and nods. The rain is, once again, a persistent drizzle and the evergreens around them sag from the slow onslaught; a fog hovers at the edge of their view, shielding the top of that tombstone-topped hill over there, that path leading down to the pond and the mausoleums, with one of the two batwing gates at the entrance.

A preacher is saying something as Ronnie ponders how they all got here.

"First, TomTom. Then his brother. Maybe we *are* cursed."

Ronnie's eyes widen. "Pick?"

"Reminds me, bruh. We gotta spend time with Mrs. Reynolds. Losing both boys like that."

Ronnie sees a withered old woman across the casket, sheltered from the rain by her plastic parasol, head bowed, weeping. Their eyes lock briefly, but Ronnie swears hers are furrowed with accusation.

* * *

His apartment door unlocks silently, and Ronnie shakes off the cold and the rain. There are fresh scratch marks on the outside door panels, blood left in a tacky rivulet, but there is no sign of her. No lights are on, so the shadows are playfully impish to his drunken mind, jumping and slinking with every glance. He relishes the cold quiet, just as the recently dead might relish their grave.

* * *

By the end, he can fit all five or her toes into his mouth, well past the arch. Ronnie cradles her heel delicately, his thumb and forefinger on either side of her Achilles. He likes to stroke her calf in her human form. They alternate feet based on what day of the week it is.

He's naked on her bed, curled up in the bend of her legs. She's naked also, turned away from him, arms tucked in and folded around her breasts. Then he's on all fours in her entryway and she stands akimbo in crotchless leather, grabbing his ears as he nuzzles up her thighs.

* * *

Mrs. Hayfield's leg still kicks a little. More like a twitch, like an electric shock quakes through it. She can barely move, save the last light of her eyes as they focus on Ronnie's face. The A-string's divot into the flesh of her neck reddens and deepens. Her breath wheezes something similar to words, and her lips twist to better articulate, but Ronnie cannot make anything out. He wonders if she expected to go like this, strangled in one of her tenant's units, taking her last breath while staring up at the popcorn ceiling she'd paid someone to spray a decade earlier.

He kneels and brushes her cheek with the backs of his fingers. The A-string is bent to hell and will never work on the fretboard now, so it lays lifeless next to her body.

"She's got to find me again," he says. "You understand, don't you?"

The old woman's bottom lip flattens, and she forces air that makes a "WH…" sound.

"Why?" Ronnie asks for her. She blinks. He reaches a hand down and wraps his fingers around her throat. "Why?" he says with a squeeze.

She punches the base of her fist on the floor and thrashes some, but these struggles are nothing against his strength. It is her settling into complacency that is his consent.

"Because you are a mean old horrible woman," Ronnie says. "I am sorry I was late those times for rent, and I'm sorry I was two weeks late this time. But goddammit I told you I had it, didn't I?" He squeezes and she gasps. "And still you kept on. Still you kept fucking on."

She reaches up weakly with a trembling hand and paws at his wrist.

"And she's got to know," he says, offering her one final smile as his fingers tighten. "She's got to know I was looking for her."

She teaches him to purr and growl and roll over. When he's completely submissive, she rubs his belly without fear of retaliation. His memories are bluish gray. Cold and analytical. She isn't there when the rescue team arrives. When he hugs his friends, he can feel her close, but can't see her. Still, he knows she's close like he knows the earth is round.

* * *

Another band is doing soundtracks that bleed through the gaps between the door and frame. The smoke and smell of beer filters through also. Ronnie shifts and Ossie pats his back. None of this goes unnoticed by the two detectives sitting across from them.

"One a' those punk bands, ain't ya?" the male detective says.

The female detective taps her pen. "So, lets talk about what happened with Ben Skids."

"We talked about that already," Ossie says.

Ossie also says this is how we address women. So many men want sex, but what they don't realize they want—"

* * *

"—what they don't realize they want," Ronnie says to the eviscerated fat, hairy stomach splayed out in front of him. "…is to love. To feel secure." He considers the rubber gloves at his knees and thinks, *I'd need them to dig through his fat and his hair-studded and greasy tummy,* but the blood-painted colon and small intestine make his mouth water. "With Ben Skids, she ate," Ronnie tells the corpse of their band manager. "And you stole. Oh, fuck it you're TomTom's cousin. We all know why you got the job."

TomTom's cousin, Oscar, can't answer. His favorite Hawaiian shirt soaks up the blood pooling at his back, his once-plump cheeks thin and gray in the fluorescent office light. All the moisture seemed to leave his body on death. Even his greasy, curly hair lay drab as

* * *

"Ben Skids was stalking y'all," the female detective says.

Ronnie looks to Ossie for confirmation before he nods.

"You asked us already," Ossie says. "Yeah, he was stalking us. Followed us to a lot of our shows—"

"And ended up dead after one of 'em," the male detective says.

I shiver at this.

"We told you," Ossie says. "We was done for the night."

"Yet a witness placed a member of your band at the scene of the crime."

Several things happen when the female detective says this. One, she shoots an accusatory glare at Ronnie, and two, Ossie rubs Ronnie's back, and three, Ronnie reaches for his guitar for comfort, and four, he remembers. Not that he ever repressed that night, but the events intrude in technicolor. Ronnie was at the scene of the crime, about to be mugged by the long-haired, leather-clad, cig-smoking dude when she arrived.

"I wasn't..." he bumbles.

"You were," the female detective says with soft, batting eyes that take up his whole field of vision.

"That's when *she* took you," her gruff partner adds.

"This isn't good for him right now," Ossie says, stretching his arm across Ronnie's chest. He's reminded of his mother making a similar movement anytime she had to slam on the brakes of their car, which was frequently; she was not a good driver.

"We have to find—"

"You can't," he interrupts. "Not when he's all riled up like this." Ronnie, having already stiffened, nearly corpselike, stares up at the yellow-stained popcorn ceiling. He sits like that until the cops leave, and Ossie shuts and locks the door. Outside, there's a distant roll of thunder and the soft pellets of rain beating down on the tin roof to suggest another storm is moving in.

Ronnie breathes hard and looks at the floor. The carpet is brown with darker splotches. It smells of both bleach and the last vestiges of decay and, if Ronnie stares hard enough, it all blends to something muddy-colored and rough-textured. "I wish they never found me."

"Man," Ossie says, and for a moment can't say more. He's appalled, almost enough to remove the plastic shades covering his eyes. "Man, naw."

"She's looking for me," Ronnie says.

"Man, no. You don't…" He stands and paces some between a yellow stain on the wall that looks like Ronnie's third grade teacher Mrs. Frump and another stain the shape of Florida, except with the peninsula flipped the other way and leading into the kitchen/dining area. "You think she out there getting' revenge 'cause you escaped? You ain't responsible."

Ronnie opens his mouth to say I am, ready to confess to the murder of their band manager and the murder of his landlady, but he hears, under the rumbles closing in, the padding of feet ascending the concrete stairs outside. He hears this not just with his ears, but also in the prickle of his flesh. His heart thuds once and the beat radiates out, catching her crouching silhouette on the other side of the door as if he is a bat with sonar.

"Ossie," Ronnie says.

"You, you mean you want her to find you?"

"Ossie," Ronnie repeats and outside, the lightning flashes and the rain falls harder, nearly as slick off the tin as sleet.

"Ronnie, listen man." He squats in front of his friend and grabs his forearms and stares up into his eyes. "You don't … I mean, you ain't got to …" He sighs and averts his eyes for a minute, his lips twitching in a silent curse. "Fuck 'member when? Fuck, when we was at lunch that one day a few months back. We was talkin' 'bout what women want in a man, or what we should want with her? Intimacy ain't just sex, man. You can't get that with her? They got a name for that, like stockweiser synopsis or some shit, but man, you can't—"

Ossie is interrupted by two sounds. The first is the sound of glass shattering but not in the room. No, instead it's muffled as if behind a door. Ronnie looks towards the closed door leading to his bedroom. The second sound is a rat-a-tat on the front door before the door jamb splinters and the two detectives, with several patrol cops, enter.

Ronnie bolts for his bedroom door as Ossie stands, hands up.

* * *

Three patrolmen push past Ossie and check Ronnie's the door with a quick jiggle of the handle.

It's locked.

The detectives slap Ossie's hands down as they pass him, annoyed as if he were a fly.

"Come out," the female detective calls, and Ossie wonders why they didn't announce themselves just now. "We know, Ronnie. Coroner confirmed COD for your landlady. Strangulation by a thin, bendable, metal wire. Said it came from an A-string off a guitar."

A female voice, very muffled, from behind the door to Ronnie's room. "You tried to frame me?"

"No," Ronnie says.

Ossie tries to step towards the door, but a uniformed cop palms his shoulder.

"I … I wanted to get your attention."

"And the bite marks, Ronnie," the female detective continues, "on your band manager. They *don't* match the bitemarks on TomTom or his brother or that Skids creep."

"You think I'm a dog," the female voice with Ronnie says. To Ossie, she sounds appalled, but the patrolman won't remove his hand and he's at least a foot and a half taller than Ossie.

Regardless, when Ronnie cries out, Ossie jumps forward, slips the grip, only to be body blocked by the male detective as two more patrolmen snatch either arm.

"You hear that!" Ossie says. "You hear her in there. She's in there."

"…access to that place," the female detective continues, ignoring Ossie. "Ronnie, it's time you come out and fess up. Your friend is here. He deserves to know the truth."

"Oh," the female voice says behind the door. "You wanna be *my* dog?" Ossie hears the smile on her lips, but this doesn't reassure him. The smile is accompanied by a tenor of cruelty.

The sound of the bed springs squeaking come, unmistakable to Ossie, and the cops exchange a glance, but surely must recognize the sound as well. The female detective motions to the patrolmen and says, "Bust it down," as, overhead, the thunder cracks and the lights about them flicker.

The hollow door splinters with a single kick. The patrolmen enter first, then the female detective. Her counterpart drags Ossie in by his ear.

Ronnie lays on the bed. He stares up at the ceiling, a glaze already icing over his eyes. Arcs of blood spray the walls. Blood bubbles from the shredded jugular. In fact, his whole neck has been exposed. Jagged bits of tissue sprinkle red across the gray bedspread.

Outside, another flash of lightning, and the interiors flash again. Ossie spies a smattering of something glittering in his periphery. It lays scattered across the bedspread and even the carpet by the wall, and he can follow its trail up to the window. The blinds flap from the storm outside. Ossie smells the rain and the grass and feels the cool of the air driving the storm.

"Oh, Ronnie," Ossie whimpers, his eyes returning back to his friend.

Suddenly, the female detective snatches him away from her partner, and she shakes Ossie so violently that his sunglasses fall off. She glares at the fear drawn on Ossie's face. "Your friend killed your band manager and his landlady," she says. "He wasn't innocent."

Her partner stretches out a level hand as she drops Ossie's collar and turns away from him. "But what about my bandmates, and that dude stalking us?"

The detective doesn't answer, but she exchanges a look with her partner that tells Ossie all he needs to know.

She doesn't know.

ROCK 'N' ROLL

SCREAMING INFIDELITIES
Brian McAuley

I'm reading your note again, trying to make sense of it all. So many standard lines, each phrase more hollow than the last.

"We want different things."

"You deserve to be happy."

But how can you love me "always and forever" if you're gone?

Six months deserves more than a note, but I know that's not your style. You prefer the easy route, no confrontation. I recognize the paper – sorry, *parchment* – you bought at that bougie boutique on the west side. You said you were gonna use it to write down your "daily intentions," but I never saw that happen. Maybe you did it in secret, just like everything else. If your intention was to destroy my life, then you manifested it well. Left me all alone in my studio apartment with nothing but this bottle of Beast to keep me company. The creature on the label bares its teeth, ready to chew me up and swallow me whole.

You always questioned why I never drank anything else. "Why don't you treat yourself to something a little more top shelf?"

See, you think I drink Beast because it's the cheapest bourbon, but that's not true. I drink it because every bar carries it. It's reliable. Loyal.

Something you wouldn't understand.

I put the bottle to my lips and tilt the whiskey down my throat, close my eyes and let it burn. Picturing myself engulfed in welcome flames, I imagine you standing there, empty gas can in hand. Watching me flail on fire with a big wide grin.

When I open my eyes again, the note looks different. There's a black scratch of ink in the corner that I hadn't noticed before. It's not like you to be so sloppy. My thumb rubs over this proof of your imperfection, and it moves at my touch.

Because it's not ink after all.

It's a strand of your hair.

Now *that's* devious. You put it there on purpose, didn't you? A little memento, just to taunt me. You know how much I love your hair. That long black mane was the first thing I saw the day we met. Drew me straight in while I was waiting in line behind you at Dashboard Café.

"Excuse me," I said. "I'm so sorry to bother you, but I have to ask. Who does your hair? It looks amazing, and I'm looking for someone who can handle mine."

"Oh, honey." You smiled and ran your fingers over my bald head. "I've got some bad news for you."

A touch and a 'honey,' right off the bat? I was putty in your hands.

Didn't stand a chance.

We spent hours at the corner table, sipping black coffee and spilling our guts. Both fresh out of five-year relationships, just getting back into the swing of online dating. Not looking for anything serious, but desperate for human heat. We even swapped phones and swiped on each other's Sizzl profiles, laughing at the flexing bros and filtered girls.

"Ooo, I think we have a winner." You showed me your own profile on my phone.

"Swipe right," I said, and you did.

Ding-ding. It's a match.

"What's your opening line?" You smiled that damn smile.

I leaned over the table, tucked your hair behind your ear, and whispered a bed-bound promise. I don't know where that confidence came from, I really don't, but the moan you made in response to my words? The way you gripped my shoulder in the packed coffeeshop?

"Prove it," you said.

We rushed back to my place as fast as our feet could carry us. The chemistry was unreal, and it wasn't just the sex. It was the way we laid in bed after, sharing battle scars and fits of laughter.

I think that's what I miss the most. The sound of your laugh.

Had it been fading all along, ever since that day? Was I just too stupid to notice?

It's quiet now, in my apartment. No trace of the passion or joy that used to echo off these walls. I pluck the hair from your note and hold it to my nose, inhaling. Your rosemary scent drifts up, even from this single strand. It's that natural shampoo you bought at the farmer's market. I used to complain every time you dragged me there at eight o'clock on Sunday mornings.

"Why would I spend fourteen dollars on a loaf of bread when it's four dollars at Trader Joe's?" I whined.

"Because this is freshly baked with no preservatives, and we're supporting a small business owner instead of some capitalist corporation."

How could I argue with your incessant altruism?

We strolled to the booth where a greying Man Bun was selling goat's milk soap bars. You bought two bottles of shampoo from him.

"Let me guess." I wrapped my arm around your shoulder as we walked away. "You buy them two at a time because the expensive organic shampoo doesn't last very long."

"No." You swatted my hand, playful. "It actually lasts longer than that mass produced chemical sludge. I just thought it might be useful if I kept a bottle at your place."

The crowd faded from my vision. I pulled you in and kissed you, right there, in the middle of the market. Strangers clapped and cheered around us as we pressed our smiles together, swimming in bliss.

It was the happiest moment of my life, I know that now.

Only in retrospect.

Only in your absence.

Your shampoo's still here, in the shower. Maybe that's what I need. A nice warm rinse to wash you off my skin.

I tuck the single hair back in your note, oh so delicately, then clench my fist around the overpriced parchment and shoot the crumpled ball into the trash. The Beast comes with me as I head into the bathroom and turn the water on hot. One more gulp from the bottle before I place it on the sink and step inside the shower.

Deep breaths flush my lungs with steam, but the pain remains.

You always said I loved to wallow. A sweet tease that took a hard turn toward concerned complaint one day when you added, "I don't think the whiskey is helping."

Well, it's helping now. I reach my arm through the curtain, grab the Beast by its neck and take another swig as the water beats against my chest.

Maybe I won't wallow tonight. Maybe I'll get myself cleaned up and head down to Saints and Sailors. Have a little fun at our favorite dive bar. Find someone to make out with, anyone at all.

It's nice to imagine, but I know it wouldn't work. I know I'd just be thinking about you, wishing I knew you were safely at home.

Home.

Your little note didn't mention it, but we both know that was the big issue. The dealbreaker. I thought it was time for us to move in together. You said you weren't ready, that you needed your own space.

Now I know why.

I thought we were building a picture-perfect life together, piece by piece, getting closer and closer to that pretty landscape on the box. The house on the hill with the warm kitchen light on. But you've left this ruined puzzle in your wake, and nothing fits anymore.

The water flows down my body into the drain, where a tangled black mass swirls in endless circles around the chrome. Maybe you didn't leave it on purpose, but you could have at least cleaned up after yourself if you knew you were going for good. I flip the water off, bend down and scoop your soggy hair from the drain. Wet like seaweed, it shimmers and shines.

And pulses.

I scramble out of the shower, tripping over the tub's edge as I throw the throbbing hair blob into the open toilet. My breath catches up to me as I peer into the white bowl. The wet black mass floats, but doesn't move. I swear I felt it twitch in my palm, though. Probably just trapped air or something.

I reach for my towel, the high thread count one you insisted on buying for us both after that targeted Instagram ad suckered you in.

"It's worth the investment," you said, "for something you use every day."

Burying my face in the plush towel now, I let it hug my cheeks and hate that you're right. It's so soft, comforting. Tears try their best to burst through my eyelids, but I won't let them. Even if these luscious threads would soak them right up.

I can't let you have that win, too.

When I pull the towel down and look in the mirror, I see the long black strand running down my cheek. It wriggles like a worm pulled from the earth. A shriek scrapes up my throat as I swipe it off my skin, into the sink. The hair sticks against porcelain, motionless.

Just another stray hair.

No, it wasn't alive.

No, it couldn't have moved.

The Beast must be playing tricks on my eyes. Two me's stare back from the mirror, all wobbly and undefined, confirming my drunken suspicions. That doesn't stop me from taking another drink, killing the dregs of my favorite medicine before I drop the empty bottle in the trash.

My fingertips scour the towel to find a few more hairs. Obsessively plucking them, I dispose of all the evidence that you ever even existed.

Did you take my towel and leave me with yours? Another sly torture? One of your best deceptions?

I toss the towel to the floor, grip the sink's edge, and hang my head. No way I can go out tonight. Definitely not to Saints and Sailors, never again. You've tainted our special place forever.

I still can't believe how bold you were. I mean, really, can you even pretend you didn't want to get caught?

It was just two nights ago you told me you weren't feeling well. I offered to come over and make you my signature spicy ramen with seitan. Satan's Soup is your favorite.

"That's really sweet." Your voice all scratchy. "But I don't want to get you sick." Such a thoughtful faker. "Besides, I'm about to pass out on NyQuil."

Then yesterday your little note arrived in my mailbox. Seriously, how cowardly do you have to be to break up through snail mail?

After I read it the first time, I blasted all the saddest songs from our "all the saddest songs" playlist until I got tired of being alone. Decided to head down to Saints and Sailors to drown my sorrows.

Our favorite bartender was working, his familiar face a small comfort.

"The usual please, Chris." I was ready to pour my heart out to him on that sticky wooden bar, but Chris looked nervous. Kept glancing over my shoulder as he poured the Beast over ice.

"Why don't we make that a double?" He pushed the glass across the bar to me. "On the house."

I followed his gaze to the back booth, and there you were.

Making out.

With him.

That goat's milk Man Bun motherfucker.

Do you have any idea what that felt like? Watching you shove your tongue down his throat while Chris watched me watching you? How humiliating it was for me?

My first instinct was to run, but I didn't. I tucked myself into the corner beside the jukebox, the one we used to play "Lips of an Angel" on while ironically singing along until everyone in the bar hated us. Maybe you weren't being so ironic after all.

The shadows kept me hidden while I leaned against the wall in a daze.

Watching.

Waiting.

Fighting the growing urge to storm straight up to your table and start screaming infidelities.

But I stayed quiet.

Stayed calm.

Snuck to the bar a couple more times when you were too face-deep in his face to see me.

Chris cut me off after my third double, which was fine, because you and Man Bun were reaching for your coats anyway. You were both so wasted that you didn't notice me following you home.

I gave you a little time to get started before I slipped into the apartment, using the key you gave me. Another reason I thought we were ready to move in together. But no, I was just reading into things, right? A meaningless gesture.

There was no plan, really, nothing premeditated. I stood in the kitchen, totally numb, no tears falling while I listened to you fuck him in the same bedroom where I just fucked you four days ago. I don't even remember pulling the big knife from the block on the counter. I bought you those knives so I could slice up all that seitan. Can't believe I went vegan for you, like an iron-deficient idiot.

The bedroom door creaked when I crept into the bedroom, but your moans masked the sound. I stood at the foot of your bed, watching him take you from behind like an animal.

Again I went unnoticed. It was so easy to grab that man bun in one hand and press the knife to his neck with the other. I made sure to tilt his head back, to look him right in the eyes. There was a flash of recognition just before I dragged the blade across his throat. Blood sprayed against your back as he stumbled off the bed, grasping at the gushing wound, doing a brilliant dance across the carpet until he bounced off the wall and collapsed to the floor.

A scream rushed up towards your lips, but my hands were already around your throat to cut it off. You fought the good fight, I'll give you that. Squirmed in my grip and scratched at my bald head. When it was all over, I laid there in bed with you one last time. Stroking your beautiful hair. Staring into your wide eyes.

I never noticed how fake they were until I saw the true you in death.

It's been twenty-four hours since I left you there. I've just been wandering my apartment like a ghost, sipping that Beast and waiting for the inevitable. Honestly, I'm surprised the cops haven't come knocking on my door already. Maybe it'll take another day or two for the stench to set in, for the neighbors to make the call. I don't expect to get away with it, I really don't. I'll tell them everything, write out my full confessional on your stupid parchment.

Spending the rest of my life in prison doesn't bother me.

The real bitter pill will be living without you.

At least I'm clean now. The blood is all washed off as I crawl into my bed, cuddling close to the blankets and sheets that could've been our blankets and sheets. I wish I could drift off to sleep and wake up to find you by my side. Mornings in bed were my favorite. Black coffee and sexy snoozes. It's so cold without you here. Funny how the happiest spaces so quickly turn dark. How the places with the warmest memories become the places that I've come to fear the most.

I run my hand along your empty pillow, and it catches like a fish in a net. More hair, all wrapped and tangled through my fingers. Where the hell is it coming from? The black spiderweb tightens around my skin, won't let me go. I pick and pull at the strands, finally freeing my fingers and tossing the tangled knot to the floor.

It laughs.

Your hair laughs your laugh just before it slinks beneath the bed.

Too scared to look, I just lie flat on my back and pull the comforter up to my nose.

The words from your note flash through my frantic mind.

"Always and forever."

Sounds less like a promise now. More like a threat.

Something tickles my toes, slithers up my calf.

My hands shake as I peek under the sheets. The black snake of pure hair glides over my stomach, up my chest. I grab the beast with both hands, but it writhes from my grip and slips between my lips. Wriggling over my tongue, down my scratchy throat. The tangled thing curls up in my stomach and fills my lungs, spreading to every corner. Leaves me just enough space to breathe, to stay alive while it happens. While the twisted strands squirm through every inch of me. Black threads weave in and out of my prickling pores, consuming me from the inside out until my whole world goes dark.

Until your hair is everywhere.

WOW
PUNK
RACHEL HARRISON
MUSIC

THIS COULD BE LOVE

Rachel Harrison

There are dead baby birds scattered along the sidewalk, their translucent bodies shining under the bright May sun. It's that time of year, the season of falling nests. The birds lie among cigarette butts and trash, among well-worn Doc Martens sidestepping their precious little corpses. Towering above them, an army of washed-up punks who knew my father, whose corpse has been freshly incinerated to ash, and who sits in the trunk of my car, parallel parked, poorly, down the block.

"You okay there, Lou?" It's Timmy Waters, former bassist of The Merry Arsonists, now the lone surviving member of one of the greatest bands to never quite make it. They were festival famous, and even played Lollapalooza, but they only managed one headlining tour. Their videos aired on late nineties/early aughts MTV. You could buy shirts with their logo at Hot Topic, but they were never Blink-182.

Not that they fucking cared.

"Was a nice eulogy. Liked that part about the matching tattoos. I didn't know that."

"Midnight on my eighteenth birthday." I flip my forearm to show off the small skull on my inner wrist with two lit matches in place of crossbones. A variation of the band's logo.

"There it is!" Timmy says, grinning. His teeth are brown from all the cigarettes and the booze and the drugs. He's supposed to be clean now, but who knows.

None of these guys are long for this world.

"He was so proud of you."

"Thanks, Timmy," I say. "I know he was."

He takes a long drag of his Marlboro Red. "Still can't believe he's gone."

"Really?" I ask, cocking an eyebrow. "He drank like a fucking fish and was a dope fiend for nine years. He was my hero, and I miss him already, but this…" I pause to gesture around. Everyone's in black— *because they always wear black, not because it's a funeral*— but my point stands. "This isn't a surprise. I've been preparing for this my whole life."

Timmy stomps out his cigarette. "Yeah, but see…that…that breaks my heart."

He kisses me on the forehead and heads back inside to pick at whatever remains of the food—soggy pasta and hard bread and romaine drowned in "Italian dressing" that's essentially straight vinegar.

I take another moment outside of this very New Jersey funeral parlor to feel the warm sunshine on my skin. It reminds me of what it was like to be near him. To be bathed in light radiating from the brightest star.

He was complicated. A stereotypical musician/addict who was always on the road, always wrestling with his demons.

"I give it all up there," he told me once, sweat drenched and breathless after a show. "Break off a piece of my soul every single time, throw it out into the crowd. Let them gnaw on it like dogs."

He opened a forty, clanked his cracked teeth against the bottle.

"You'll always be my number one, though," he said, winking. "You're the best of me, Lou. Best thing I've ever done."

Then he got stone-faced, stared out at nothing.

"Hope you never know about the worst."

Of course, I knew about the worst. There were syringes on the tour bus. He contracted hepatitis C. Five years ago he passed out smoking a cigarette in bed and burned his house down.

I loved my father. My father loved me. But he was hopelessly self-destructive. More than anything, I think he loved to set things on fire just to watch them burn.

In a sense, it brings me comfort, to know he's now ash.

* * *

Dad's still in my trunk when I drive from the hotel to his apartment the next morning. I get lost twice. I've never been to this place. I'd been to his old house once or twice before it burned down, but mostly he would come to see me, or I'd be on the road with him, on the bus.

Mom offered to hire someone to do this, to clean out his apartment, but I didn't want strangers touching Dad's shit.

My parents' love story wasn't one. They met at a show in some grungy Lower East Side venue that doesn't exist anymore, hooked up, tried a long-distance romance while Dad toured and Mom got her bachelor's at NYU. It didn't work out. They tried again. I came along. It didn't work out for the second time. Or third. Or twenty-third. Mom moved on with Ken, a tax attorney who whisked us off to Westport, Connecticut. I got to have a normal, boring suburban childhood, occasionally punctuated by whirlwind visits with my fun-loving rockstar father.

Mom and Dad never got along, never settled into a healthy coparenting rhythm. Dad wasn't reliable. Mom resented him. Still, I was a little disappointed when she opted out of attending his funeral.

"I love that you loved him," she'd said. "But he put me through a lot."

In lieu of emotional support, she gave financial. She paid for my travel—gas, the hotel, and had I accepted, a cleaning service. Dad was always insecure about how he couldn't contribute, money-wise.

"If I had it, I'd give it," he'd say.

There were so many times I almost told him how I didn't care. That I resented my stepfather's attempts to buy my affection, and begrudged my mother's concerted efforts to prove herself the superior parent, undermining my father through giving me a "good life."

But I always held my tongue, because as enamored as I was with Dad, I was grounded enough to understand that I was lucky to have my mom and

Ken, grateful for the comfort and stability they provided me. To dismiss their sacrifices would be a betrayal.

Now that he's gone, I wish he knew it didn't matter to me, that he never sent me gifts or bought me clothes or paid tuition or anything. He gave me experiences. Let me stay up until dawn listening to records, sleeping through the afternoon. He let me eat hamburgers for breakfast and waffles for dinner. Taught me how to play guitar and roll cigarettes and throw a right hook and make coffee with toilet paper as a filter and to spit like a cowboy and to curse like a fucking sailor.

The GPS informs me I've now arrived at my destination, and I pull up to a rundown complex on the side of the road.

There are a few parking spots out front, the lines faint, pavement cracked. I take an open spot and hope it's not assigned.

Getting out of the car, there's a whiff of trash and I notice a dumpster on the other side of the lot. It's overflowing.

My heart is heavy, knowing this is where he spent the last years of his life. The last moments of his life. Went to bed, never woke up. Died in his sleep. A lucky break for an unlucky enterprise.

"Hey." There's a woman in a threadbare robe smoking a cigarette on her balcony. She sits in a beach chair, uses a flowerpot as an ashtray even though there are wilting pansies still inside. Her hair's silver and wild, her eyes hidden behind massive black sunglasses.

"Morning," I say. "There are no assigned spots, are there? I'm just here to clean out my dad's place."

"Lou?" she asks, dropping her sunglasses to get a better look at me.

"Yeah," I say. "I'm Lou."

"Sorry about your dad. We all loved Mikey around here. A shame. All the good ones croak, and the shit stains hang around forever."

"So it goes," I say.

She takes a drag. "Well. Your car's fine there, other than it might get stolen."

"Great," I say, saluting her as I fumble the apartment keys out of my pocket. The bigger one gets me into the building. I climb the stairs up to the second floor, looking for his unit. 3B.

I take a deep breath before unlocking the door.

It reeks. Like cigarettes and…I don't know what that smell is. Death?

He wasn't rotting here. His sponsor, Sean, found him the next day. Dad had texted him the night before, making plans to meet for breakfast. When Dad didn't show, Sean came by for a wellness check and discovered things were not too well.

I walk over to the kitchenette and open the fridge. The stench that comes wafting out is beyond rancid. I slam the door shut but it's too late. I vomit into the sink.

"Fuck." I wipe my mouth on a paper towel, swatting away fruit flies as I stumble out of the kitchen, into the rest of the living space.

The walls are completely papered in posters—mostly of bands he loved, but I spy a faded vintage *Creature from the Black Lagoon* print, his all-time favorite movie. Mr. Tattooed Tough Punk had a soft spot for misunderstood monsters. His guitars are hung up on hooks, glimmering like trophies. Amps and pedals crowd the corner. There are books and albums and old magazines stacked from floor-to-ceiling. His prized record player rests on a table, covered in a black sheet patterned with white skulls. There's a beat-up leather couch in the middle of the room. A transistor radio on the floor. A lamp with its tasseled shade askew. There's a short hallway. To the left, a tiny bathroom with yellowed tile and a glass cell of a shower; to the right, Dad's bedroom. A glorified closet that fits a queen mattress on a box spring and a dresser overflowing with black jeans and t-shirts.

It's too much for me to stare at his unmade bed, the ghost of his shape in the sheets, so I walk back into the living room, wondering if I have it in me to clear this place out after all.

Still nauseous from the smell, I collapse onto the couch and take a moment to think, make a game plan.

"All right," I say to myself. I stand, walk over to the lone window, and crack it open. It's not the freshest air, carrying with it the scent of dumpster garbage, but it's something.

Then I walk over to the record player. I'll put on some music. Take out his guitars first—the instruments most precious to him, now most precious to me.

My foot connects with something under the table, beneath the skull patterned sheet.

A cry of static.

I crouch down, worried I broke something. I carefully peel back the sheet.

There's an ancient, boxy TV hiding under there. A TV so old it has a VHS player. Beside it, a cardboard box full of tapes.

"Huh," I say, pulling out the TV and the unlabeled tapes.

The static persists until suddenly, jarringly, it's my father.

Dad. And The Merry Arsonists.

They jam out in a graveyard, singing about last night's decisions coming back to haunt them.

It's the music video for their song "Hangover".

At the end of the video, the band climbs up on gallows that appear beyond the headstones, stick their heads in the nooses, and drop.

They were known for being morbid, which was all thanks to Dad. He'd had a fascination with the macabre ever since he was a kid, after he watched his best friend get flattened by a car while chasing a ball into the street, a story Dad told me once and only once, drunk and laughing until he was dead-eyed sober.

The TV goes static again and I eject the tape.

This one is labeled, with black Sharpie, in Dad's chaotic script. "MTV bullshit".

A grin spreads wide across my face as I trace my fingers over his writing, and for a moment I feel nothing but love, pure and transcendent. This is it. What makes me grateful for the grief, the pain of his absence. This boundless, enduring love for my father. I know it could be enough to get me through. It has to be.

I set the tape aside and reach into the box for another. I pop it in and press play, cross my legs and lean back, anticipating more archival footage of The Merry Arsonists.

What comes up on the screen confuses me.

The image is grainy. It's a cheap motel room. There's a woman. She's in a white lace slip. Barefoot. Gagged and bound. Facedown on the bed.

She struggles against her bindings, but she's tied too tight to sit upright. She flips over instead.

She's box blonde with dark roots. She wears excessive, clown-like makeup. Dark blue eyeshadow, berry lipstick, hot pink blush, all smudged. She's been crying, and mascara runs down her cheeks.

There are track marks on her arms. Bruises.

Her eyes are bloodshot. Pleading.

What is this?

The camera zooms out, showing more of the dingy room. There's another queen bed, just barely in view. A fluorescent light blinks on in the bathroom, the door is open and there's movement in the mirror, the cameraman almost caught in frame. I debate rewinding, pausing to see if I can identify him, and I almost miss the emergence. The gloved hand reaching out from under the bed. But then the camera angles down, shakily, and I choke on my exhale as I watch a man crawl across the floor, darkness flaking away as he leaves the shadows beneath the mattress behind. He wears gardening gloves, a white sweatshirt, black jeans, and no shoes. Just socks. He has a burlap sack over his head, black scribbles where his eyes should be. He stands up at the foot of the bed.

There's no sound except the woman's muffled cries.

The man has a knife in his hand.

What the fuck is this?

A music video shot and rejected?

I want to believe that, but it's too obvious that this would never play. It's too disturbing.

Even Dad would know that.

So then why does he have it?

The man starts dancing around, waving the knife over his head. He circles the bed, picking up his knees, kicking his legs, swiveling his hips. It's a distinct style of movement.

It's the way my father would dance, sometimes. On stage. The audience would follow suit. Mimic him. But I've seen people do it at other shows, too, dancing to other bands over the years. It's not just a Dad thing. Not just a Merry Arsonists thing.

The man switches it up. Starts doing the twist.

I think, I hope, that maybe this will be the moment when things shift.

That the terror will wither. That this is about to take a welcome turn into fun horror camp.

But then the man grabs a fistful of the woman's hair and pulls her head up. He drags her off the bed and to the other queen, which is covered in black trash bags.

I don't want to keep watching, but I need to know what happens. I need to see. I need fake blood. Some proof that this isn't what I fear it is.

The woman bucks, fights against the man. She manages to wriggle her hands free, the rope binding her falling away. She scratches at the man, but he's protected, every inch of him covered in fabric. Even his mouth. The burlap sack sinks and swells with his breath. He catches one of her wrists and slashes the knife across her hand, severing her fingers.

She falls back onto the bed, eyes wide in shock.

Her middle and ring fingers are sliced to the bone. Her pinky is gone. It's off.

The man climbs onto the bed and removes her gag. She laughs.

She's laughing.

And I wonder if I should be laughing. I wonder what about this is funny. What am I missing? When will it make sense?

I lean forward, trying to get a better look at the woman's injuries, to see if they're real or if it's fake gore.

I'm about to press pause when the masked man slowly, methodically drags the blade across the woman's throat.

Blood soaks her white lace slip. It doesn't spray out like a cheap special effect. It's almost graceful, the way it spills from the wound. Like a busy river.

The masked man holds the bloody knife behind his back as he watches the woman bleed out. Her eyelids droop shut. Her body goes limp.

She's dead.

I just watched her die.

I just witnessed a murder.

This is a snuff film.

The man reaches down with a gloved hand, swirling his finger through the growing puddle of blood forming beneath the woman, on top of the garbage bags.

I smash my fist into the VCR control panel. The screen goes black, but I can still see it. I close my eyes, and the video plays there.

It's too hot in this apartment. The air too thick. Too rancid.

I'm going to be sick again, but I can't move.

Vomit dribbles down my chin, I wipe it away with the back of my hand.

I lunge for the box of tapes, my frantic grasp tipping it over.

There are so many. So many tapes. And…

Wads of cash line the bottom of the box. Crinkled bills. Hundreds.

If I had it, I'd give it, he always used to say.

You're the best of me, Lou. Best thing I've ever done.

Hope you never know about the worst.

* * *

The tapes are in the trunk with Dad.

I sit in the parking lot, in the shadow of his building, hands shaking so violently that I can't do anything. My fingers—*not severed, not flopping loose at the knuckle, not like hers*—won't cooperate, won't type "police station" into the search bar on my phone screen.

That VHS is evidence of a crime, of a murder. Who was that woman? Does she have family looking for her? Wondering what happened to her? Will it bring those who loved her peace to know how she died? I don't know. Probably not.

And God fucking knows what's on those other tapes.

It's the right thing to do, to turn them in.

So why am I feeling this intense hesitation? This pull, like a leash.

I mean, I hate the police.

Fuck the police.

But that's not why.

The scent of hot garbage and cigarettes seeps in through the cracked windows.

I have to get out of here.

I reach forward and press the button to start the car.

Music blares from the speakers.

The Merry Arsonists.

Dad's voice. He's singing to me.

Cut out my heart for you, call it love it you let me

Goodnight good morning sunshine, go on and forget me

With his voice in my ears, in my head, in my goddamn soul, I understand that I won't be taking those tapes to the police. Because I don't know if my father just had them, or if he made them. And I don't ever want to know. Or for anyone else to.

It would destroy his legacy. Taint the joy he gave to the world.

It would ruin my fucking life, if it hasn't already.

I move to turn off the music.

I turn it up instead.

* * *

There are some campgrounds out in the Pine Barrens—home of the Jersey Devil and mafia corpses and various other folklore ghouls.

I could have found somewhere else to burn the tapes, but for some reason, I felt I needed to do it here. The Pinelands feel ancient, otherworldly. They can swallow this kind of evil. It won't be their first wicked secret, and it certainly won't be their last.

My father taught me how to build a fire. He taught me how to burn.

So, I burn. The tapes. The money, because if only he knew, it never mattered to me.

I watch the tapes contort, melt into the dark heart of the flames. I throw Dad in, too. The plastic bag that's been his home for the last few days.

"Ashes to ashes," I tell him.

I'm tempted to hold my wrist over the fire, burn away the tattoo that will forever remind me of him. Maybe there'd be something poetic about it, about the matches, the very symbol celebrating arson, destruction, getting blistered and charred to obscurity. But then the scar would remind me just the same.

Maybe I'll get it covered up, change it into something else. Do my best to erase his presence. Convince myself he was never part of my life, never part of me.

Maybe tomorrow I'll wake to birdsong and the sweet scent of spring, to the beauty of nature, to a future where this memory is nothing but dust.

Or I'll wake stinking of fire, my hands dirty with my father's sins. I'll find some creek to wash them off in, but they won't get clean, will never get clean. I'll scrub my skin until I bleed, all the way down to the bone, and there he'll be, until I'm gone. Until I'm nothing. Until I'm dust.

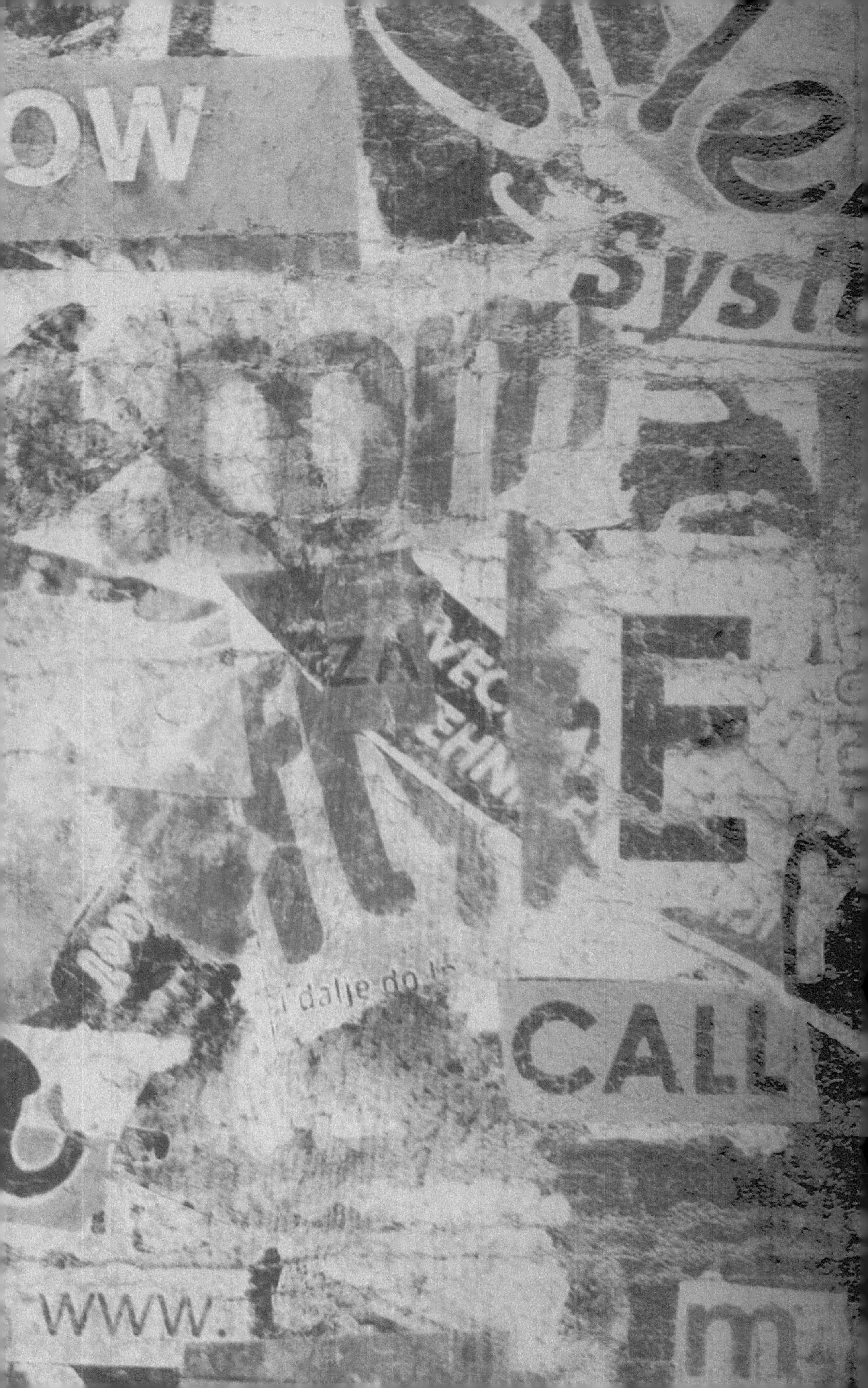

ow

Syst

i dalje do

CALL

www.

ABOUT THE EDITOR

William Sterling is an author, editor, podcaster, screenwriter, and apparently an actor now (?). Despite his inability to focus on any one trade, he is proudly, always and forever, keeping his lens trained on the spooky things.

William Sterling has published multiple novels with mid-sized presses, including *STRING THEM UP* with Crystal Lake Entertainment in 2023 and *DEAD MENS CHESTS* through Hedone Press in 2024. He has had works included in multiple anthologies, including the Stokercon - aligned Charity Anthology *SHADOWS IN THE STACKS*. He hosts the Killer Mediums podcast, is a reoccurring member of the Redwall read-along Books and Badgers podcast, and his first short film, *CANDY,* is currently in post-production. Lastly, but certainly not leastly, he is THRILLED to be releasing *PUNK goes HORROR*, for Truborn Press in March 2025.

https://thewilliamsterling.wixsite.com/main

A NOTE FROM THE PUBLISHER

We want to thank our readers for their support and enthusiasm. Your passion for stories fuels our commitment to bring you the horror that is strange and horrifying in the best of ways.

We appreciate any and all reviews, so help us out by leaving your thoughts online.

Thank you again for spending your time with us and remember to…

Follow us everywhere: @trubornpress

www.trubornpress.com

CONTENT WARNINGS

Substance Abuse

Violence

Death and Gore

Mental Health Challenges

Child Abuse and Neglect

Explicit Language

Sexual Situations

Oppression and Inequality

Supernatural Elements

Body Horror